An Eye For An Eye

An Eye For An Eye

PATRICIA MARSHALL

Order this book online at www.trafford.com
or email orders@trafford.com

Most Trafford titles are also available at major online book retailers.

Printed in the United States of America.

ISBN: 978-1-4269-5250-0 (sc)
ISBN: 978-1-4269-5252-4 (e)

Trafford rev.12/17/2010

 www.trafford.com

North America & International
toll-free: 1 888 232 4444 (USA & Canada)
phone: 250 383 6864 ◆ fax: 812 355 4082

Dedicated to my family,
who believed in me

CONTENTS

Chapter 1

It was late in the evening and Doctor Gail McDougal was just settling in for the night. It had been a long day and she deserved some down time. The holiday's would be coming up soon and it was her favorite time of year. Christmas was the very best of her childhood memories. Gail's father's birthday was Christmas Eve and so everyone, and she ment everyone, went to Mom and Dad's on the 24th. After everyone celebrated with Dad, all of the sisters and brothers went to a few Nursing homes and sang Christmas carols for the residents there. They would then return to Mom and Dad's and had sugar cookies and hot chocolate, (some had something a little stronger in their mugs). They also had a very special visitor from the north, yes; Santa would show up and Oh' how the childrens eyes would light up, they would all gather around sitting on the floor and waiting for their turn with the Jolly Old Elf. There is nothing that captures your heart, as when you see the childrens eye's glaze over in Awe, when they still believe. I still believe, because if you don't you get underware for Christmas. Ho, Ho, Ho! The McDougal's would then take the children to Midnight Mass at St. Mary's in Alton, Illinois. If you have ever been, you would know the love you feel in your heart when you left there. Memories are the joy's of growing older. Gail needed to hold onto the good ones, that's what kept her warm inside.

Married and divorced twice, by adulterous husbands, Gail still held out hope of a true love to come her way. She thought that if she gave everything to her marriage and family that things would be fine but, alas it wasn't to be.

Gail came from a very large family of eighteen children, 9 boys and 9 girls. Her mother had the patients of Job, she had to, and they are all still living except for their older brother Wayne who passed away from a heart attack two years ago. Growing up times were hard and money was short, but we always had what we needed. Maybe not the best clothes or the finest homes, but love was always bountiful. As long as Gail could remember the whole family always sat down for meals at the same time. Gail's father Elmer was served first, then the children and then their mother. No one ever came away from the table hungry.

Bedrooms were wall to wall beds, you just kept moving until it stopped and there you slept. The girls had a room and the boys had a room, same thing wall to wall. If you had to get up to use the bathroom, (which was outside) everyone went at the same time. Sometimes when it was very cold their mother had a five gallon bucket for everyone to use and then it was emptied first thing in the morning.

From all the memories Gail had her father alway's worked two full time jobs, constuction in the day and a night watchman at night at the Mississippi Lime Company. Dad would take one of us down at a time underground to see all the small little towns down there. You would have to see it to believe it. Maybe we didn't have everything but, how many rich kids got a chance to do that with their Dad. It was their one on one time with our Dad. Maybe they didn't have everything, but he made them feel as if they wern't poor at all.

Elmer would put out a four acre garden every year. March 17th no matter what the weather, Dad was out in the rain, snow, sleet it didn't matter he planted potatos on St. Patrick's Day. He said it was a family tradition to plant potatos on that day. His parent's coming from Germany and Ireland, so yes some of them had red hair and some had black and all in betwen.

They all had the temper also, they knew that they had to learn to control it. They would can vegetables and fruits all summer long and eat on it all winter long. They also raised their own beef, pork and chicken's, so they had fresh eggs for when we needed them. Gails family loved their breakfast time, they would have canned fruits or oatmeal and toast made from homemade bread. Many times at school other children wanted to trade their bologna sandwiches for our butter and jelly on homemade bread, they thought that they were eating high on the hog on those days.

Gail's parent's were from a very strong and a very Catholic family, you probably already guessed that with how many children Gail's family had. They worked from sunup to sunset and Gail thought that she inherited that trait too. So many children think that their parents owe them a living because they brought them into this world. I guess they could take them out as well... (just kidding). Men and women of the 1920-1960 had a lot different work ethics then the children of today. Gail personally thought things started to go wrong when they took prayer out of the schools and parenting out of the home. Gail and her siblings got their backsides smacked every once in a while and it never scarred any of us, well maybe my brother Harold, but he burned the barn down, full of hay and Dad's blue ribbon beagles and their puppy's. He was the only one that Gail's father ever spanked. Their mother would pick up the hair brush and like it had a homing device in it, would get you every time, They even bobbed and weaved but she still got you. All of them only had to hear their dad's voice and that's all it took.

The McDougal's were a very proud family and would never accept any charity from anyone. Monsignor Suddus at St. Mary's would buy each of the children two uniforms per child at the beginning of each school year; we had to take them off as soon as we got home so we could wear them again the next day. The McDougal children had to work in the church every day after school and on Saturday's, cleaning candles Ironing robes whatever needed done. Gail felt that helping, caring and sharing were words to live by then, and still does to this very day. Gail worked and put herself through school, and had to work hard to do it. Her second husband David went to school while Gail worked and payed the bill's, putting off her own dreams for his. Once he got his degree in computor Tecnologies he left her for another woman. "Linda" was suppose to be a very Christian woman. How many Christian woman takes another's husband? Gail also found out that David had a five year old with this woman, Gail and David were married seven years, you do the math. To David it was all about the all mighty dollar. Gail's family was her solid rock, alway's there when needed, her comfort zone.

Chapter 2

   Gail settled in for the night after locking all the doors and windows. A very large glass of wine, a little Kenny G and a good book and she was good to go. Gail made it her routine that every time she opened a book, she would say her prayer's for the night, it was her down time and you can never pray too much. Everyone needs prayer weather they know it or not. She had her book and wine and was just settling in to the comfort zone and she thought this is so nice, until the phone rang. Who could that be, she wasn't on call at the hospital. Maybe it was Katie or Steven her two children, she would have to get that now for sure, she could feel that something was wrong. "Hello; Dr. McDougal! Gail?, it's Ray and I need to speak to you so I'll be there in about 30 minutes. Her heart said yes but her mind said no, she never got the chance to decide, Ray had already hung up the phone. Gail was trying to sort out her feelings for Ray.

Gail had met Ray at a Doctor's seminar in September of 2008 at the Ritz Carlton in Clayton, Mo. Gail there to hear one of her favorite neurological surgeons in the world who was a specialist in the brain, and Ray was the caterer. Ray owned and and operated a large Catering Company for 17 years and had made quite a name for him. They met when Gail was trying to figure out what the ice sculpture could be. Ray walked up behind her and and said; close your eyes and picture a place where the waters are so blue and clear, and fragrances of flowers fill the air, and you will be there with nothing to do but enjoy it.

Gail opened her eyes and said " I don't think that this is evan close to what you just described", but it was a nice thought. It turned out to be, though slightly melted, the inside of the brain without the skull attached, after all it was a top notch neurosurgeon speaking tonight about new tactics, theories about brain changes and what they as Doctors could do to learn more. Ray asked her if she was here with her husband and then he blushed when Gail told him that she too was also a surgeon herself.

After sitting in a coffee shop talking till dawn, a bond had formed between the two of them. After that they saw each other as much as possible, 2 to 3 times a week if possible. They both had demanding jobs. Gail's office hours and then rounds at the hospital took up 14-16 hours a day, and Ray worked mainly nights, it's what the job called for. Gail had to work her way through years of schooling at Washington University and two years at St. Louis University school of Medicine. While going to Washington University she also worked while her husband David, was in school also for Computor Technologies, he didn't have time to work a part time job he said but, he sure had time to get some hooker pregnant. Gail had only time to eat and sleep a little if she was lucky. Ray had gone to Cordon Blue school in Colorado, where he learned from the best. He was very proud to be where he was today. Ray was also from a working class family, his father paid for his schooling, but Ray had him paid back within a year of his business starting off. A Catholic family originally from Sicily, they don't get more Catholic than that.

Gail hoped that Ray wasn't coming over with added stress to her life about marriage, babies and so forth. They talked about it this many times and she wasn't changing her mind. Gail heard his car pull up then the closing of the door. It took no time for Ray to come up the stairs and to her front door. Opening the door to greet him, Gail saw something in Ray's eyes that she could not miss. Ray was terrified and his face was as white as a sheet, He'd also been crying. Gail took Ray in and set him down and went and got him a glass of Brandy, which he drank straight down, Gail poured him another and then let him settle down for a moment. Ray looked into Gail's eyes and with tears in his own said; my father has had a stroke or something and it's not looking good at this point, he's at St. Louis University Hospital. I know it's a very good hospital, but do you think you could talk to the Doctors' for us and let us know what's been going on? Gail agreed to go with him, of course, only she would be doing the driving. Ray's nerves were shot and he didn't need to drive anymore tonight. As they got into Gail's car and were on their way, Ray sat there not saying a word, with his head laid back on the headrest. Gail started thinking about the first time she had met Ray's family.

Chapter 3

Gail met Mr. and Mrs. Bertolli after only two months of dating Ray. His mother, Christina and father, Michael were two people who have been in love all their lives, 55 years if you had to count them they alway's said. Raising two sons, and three daughters, they were very devoted to each other. Mr. Bertolli owned and operated a butcher shop and small store down on Market Street in St. Louis for fourty years. Christina and the three daughters, Angelina, Maria and Joelina worked in the store stocking shelves and waiting on customers, while Ray and his brother Roberto were doing deliveries to ones who couldn't make it to the store, who still does that?

Roberto was the older of the two boys by three years. After graduating from high school Roberto wanted to go back to Sicily and learn of his family from across the waters as he called it. Christina did not want him to go but held her tongue. Mr. Bertolli said it might take a little attitude out of him, after all he would be staying with his two Uncles, Dominic and Vincent, Michael's younger brothers. Roberto was very high strung and wanted to go over there for just one year, and then come back and help out in the store, he felt that college was not for him. While he was in Sicily, Roberto got a job working in the Zoo there, he took classes and worked hands on with the big cats, Tigers, Lions, Leopards and Panthers. Roberto loved it so much that he applied for and got a job working at the St. Louis Zoo working with the big cats there also. While still in Sicily, Roberto met and married a girl named Lucinda Cabello, a beautiful woman with long dark brown curly hair and very green eyes. Roberto brought her home along with one 6 month old son, Angelo. Roberto and Lucinda's brother Sonny, never got along from the beginning and Sonny was very upset that his sister married Roberto and was moving to the States. He alway's told Lucinda that she was too good for someone like Roberto. Sonny alway's wanted to boss around Lucinda and her mother every since their father had passed away two years ago. Sonny tried lying to his sister saying that Roberto was cheating on her and many other things. When Lucinda didn't beleive any of them and moved away with Roberto, that made Sonny twice as mad.

After coming back to St. Louis, they had a daughter Helena who looked just like her mother, then another son Lucas, who was his father all over again said Christina. Roberto helped in the store when he could but he had a full time job at the Zoo. He loved all of the cats but his favorites were the leopards and after only one year, the Zoo put him in charge of the Leopards Den. Roberto told Lucinda that now he was fully blessed with everything he had now, a loving family and a job he loved.

Ray was a charmer from the start; Christina said the day he was born that he had all of the nurse's under his spell. Maybe that's why I still hang on thought Gail. Anyway, Ray went from high school to two years of business study at Columbia University in Columbia Missouri. He came home every weekend to help out in the store. Ray loved to cook and knew that to be great at it, he had to be business oriented if he was going to be a Chef and own his own business, that was Ray's dream. Ray's parents gave him ten thousand dollars to start off his new business and get it off the ground. Ray had them paid back in just one year of running his successful business. Ray also bought all he needed for his company from his parents store. Ray asked his father once how he got the money to loan it to him, and his father told him that it wasn't anything and not to worry about it, he said, family takes care of family that's all that matters.

Ray had been married to a beautiful woman named Vanessa, they had met in Colorado. She was there to take pastry and souse chef classes and Ray there to take them all. Ray wanted to know everything about cooking whether it was for two people or two thousand, he always loved a challenge. When Ray brought her home, everyone loved her and she was great, Ray knew that he had made the right choice. Vanessa was a tall brunette with green eyes like the sea. Five years after they were married, Vanessa told Ray that he was going to be a father. Everyone in his family was overjoyed. Ray fixed up the nursery once they found out that it was a girl, he put little Fairy's and glitter all over the walls to welcome her home. Ray never got that chance. Ray and Vanessa were married six years when a drunk driver crossed the center lane and killed Vanessa and the baby. Ray never got to hold his daughter before they put them in the ground together. Gail could tell that Ray had a hard time with it even to this day, but he kept up a good front. He loved playing with his nieces and nephews very much, but still held out hope for us, maybe adopt a child. That was one of the things that Ray and Gail needed to talk about and soon.

Angelina was the oldest of the three girls. She had met and married a man named John Bolloer, who is an investment banker; they have five children; Jonny 12, James 10, Raymond 8, Cecillia 5, and Anna 2. Angelina had her mother's eyes and coal black hair. Their daughters looked like their mother and Jonny looked like his dad, while James and Raymond took after their uncles Roberto and Ray. Angelina and John met in the market and fell head over heels in love; John seemed to come into the market every day until he got up the nerve to ask her out. Pappa said yes that she could (after he had John checked out of cource). Everything else is history now, they were married at St. Peter & Paul's Catholic church in Alton, Illinois. John's family went to church there, as long as it was Catholic it didn't make any difference. Their oldest son Jonny, played basketball for St. Ambrose school and they went to all of their childrens games. Jonny was so tall, like his father, that they passed the ball to him a lot. James is the next oldest and couldn't be more different. James liked to take things apart, to see how it worked and then put them back together again, he also loved to paint. John said that maybe someday James would be an architect and support his parents in their old age. Raymond, named after his Uncle, loved football. He watched the game every Sunday with his dad, both were Dallas Cowboy's fans and got a lot of razing about it from others but, they didn't care. That was Raymond and John's father and son time. Cecillia was a little ballerina, and for a long time she wouldn't take off her tutu unless it was to take a bath. They had to buy four more tutu's just to be able to have a nice one for her recitals. Cecillia was to be in the Nutcraker this fall, so lots of home practices. Thank God, Anna was only two, Angelina and John felt like they were coming and going all the time. When Anna got old enough to do things, Jonny should be able to drive and could help out with some of their scheduling other to his own. They had moved just a couple blocks away from the Market so Angelina could take the children to see Nana and Poppe, somehow they always came home with candy in their pockets.

Maria's husband is Eric Guign'e, is a stock brocker at Smith and Barney in downtown St. Louis; they have two boy's Michael 11, named after his Grandpa and Daniel 8 a straight A student, a no joke man he says, wants to be a buisness man like his father. Eric asked Maria, am I a no joke man? Maria patted his hand and said you try sweetie, then they both started laughing. Melissa was 4 and looked just like her Aunt Joelina. Eric could not believe his luck. Maria looked just like a china doll, long black hair, skin so fair it was like a porcelain doll. Again after Michael checked Eric out Maria was allowed to see him. After many months of dating, Maria said yes to Eric's proposal. They live in Town & Country, only about

15 minutes from downtown St. Louis. Eric was a great father, he would take the kids to the park or Zoo to see Uncle Roberto while Maria got some good down time.Maria worked at the soup kitchen at their church. Their children went to St. Ambrose like their cousins. Eric said that being with his children was his down time, because children make life simple, you can always find a way to please a child. Their oldest Michael loved skateboarding big time. Maria thought that it was too dangerous and could not go to watch, Eric alway's had to go with him. Daniel was into roller bladeing and again it was hard for Maria to watch. Now Melissa, she wanted nothing to do with frilly things. She is a tom boy and and loves to play in the dirt, she played with the boys trucks and cars, crashing them together and just laughing her head off. Maria hopes that someday she will change her mind, either that or get used to going to the county fairs for the truck and tractor pulls.

Joelina still lived at home with her parents, working the store and taking night classes for her Masters degree in buisness. Joelina loved the store and wanted some day to take it over for her parents and take the burden off of them. They needed to have some fun while they were in good health she would tell them. The store was and still is alway's busy, Joelina at age 20 was a good mix of her parents. Her hair was very dark with some natural highlights, and the most beautiful hazel/brown eyes. One thing about Joelina, you alway's knew where you stood with her on anything, she was not shy at all. Mr. Bertolli said that she was like her Grandpa Max, very hot tempered, yet could turn to honey in a second when needed to. Michael told Christina that they would have to keep their eyes on this one; of this he had no doubt.

Chapter 4

From the first meal at Ray's parents house, (which was awesome) all anyone talked about was marriage and children for Ray and Gail. Because they had discussed these things before Ray knew how Gail felt and was okay with that he would tell her, I love you for you. After two failed marriages, annulled by the Catholic church, and two grown children, Ray said that he knew that going in and still loved Gail for herself.

Gails oldest was a daughter (Katie) was her first born, and is now a great lady. Gail had her at the age of sixteen, so it was like growing up with a lot of brothers and sisters. Katie is 21 and works in Chicago, Illinois as one of the top designers around there. Katie could look at something and change it to look like she wanted. She has a natural talent for a lot of things. Katie came into this world screaming and two weeks late, maybe that's why if Gail wanted her to be at Gail's house she would tell Katie to be there two hours earlier so she would be on time, buy it all works out somehow. Katie is very petite and looks like both of her parents, just a lot more beautiful.

Gails son's name is Steven, now 20 was two weeks early and ready for anything. Being over two pounds heavier than Katie and alway's seemed to be hungry. With dark brown eyes and very blonde hair, he was perfect. A very prompt and bright boy, he turned into a very smart man. From high school, he went into the Marines, one of the scariest things in Gail's life, with everything going on in Iraq at the time with Saddam Hussien, Gail prayed a lot. When he got out of the Marines, he went straight into being a Police officer in Jersey County and lived only about six blocks from Gail. Their town was is a small town called Hickory Grove, a place where they rolled up the street's at night and raised the flag at dawn, a small town with small town values. Gail loved going to a mom and pop store called Sinclairs. Gail had one of her knees operated on and while she was still on crutches,she had to do some shopping, they sat her down in a chair and took her grocery list and done her shopping for her, if they had any questions, they would come up and ask her. They then bagged her groceries and took them to her car and then had a cart boy follow her home and carry them into the house for her. Gail tryed to tip the young man, but he would not accept it. I don't think that you can get that kind of service anywhere else in the world. It makes you all warm inside and tears in your eyes. People come from miles away just to buy one of their homemade cakes, and they are worth every bite. Gail was still accepted to the Bertolli family, sure at times the questions came up now and then, but were alway's defused by Ray or Gail, they got very good at changeing the subjects.

Chapter 5

As Gail pulled into the hospital parking lot, she saw that her parking spot was still empty so she got to park close to the entrance. While she was parking she saw a man in a long trench coat. It was September and still warm weather, why would he be wearing that heavy coat on? When they got out of the car Gail asked Ray if he noticed that man.Ray just thought he was weird. I don't think Ray had anything on his mind but his father. Walking down the hall to the ICU department was quiet, neither one spoke until they got to the nurses station. Mary the head of ICU was doing paper work, when they walked up she stood up to greet them. Mary had a strange look on her face and Gail asked her what was wrong. She pointed to room 4 and said that the whole family was inside. Ray and Gail walked slowly to the room. Christina was in shambles, holding Michael's hand and praying. She held a rosary in the other hand and seemed like she was in shock, just going through the motions.

Ray's brother and sisters were all their also. Gail looked around and saw two people that she had never seen before. Gail looked at Ray and he whispered that they were his Uncles Dominic and Vincient Bertolli. Gail wondered why they stood at the head of the bed, one on each side, like they were guarding Michael. While Ray was with his family, Gail went out to get Mr. Bertolli's chart. Talking to Mary, she told Gail that his doctors, Dr. Michael Mucci and Dr. Edward Litzey had the chart and were in the cafeteria. Gail decided to go and have a talk with them, they were both excellent in their field of Cardiology, Heart and Vascular, Gail had studied under them when she was in school, She let Ray know where she was going.

Gail found them looking over Mr. Bertolli's chart and Lab results and thier faces were drawn as in deep thought. Gail walked up and greeted them and ask them if it would be alright if she could also be on board with their patient, She told them that the family had asked her to, Gail told them that she was dating one of Mr. Bertolli's sons, Raymond. Both doctors was happy to have a neurosurgeon on board. Like Gail, they had patients come to see them as a Primary Care Doctor, and they would see them still. Gail had about twenty or so that she still seen, and three of them were in the hospital here now.

The doctors were discussing the lab results and asked Gail to have a look at them, things were very strange about them. It seemed that someone had given Mr. Bertolli a small dose of Potassium Chloride, and his family said that he only takes Tylonol P.M. sometimes to help him sleep better and relax a little. It seemed that someone didn't want Michael around anymore. Potassium Chloried is what they give to people on death row to end their lives, and in much larger doses. When Michael was brought into the Emergency Room, he had face swelling, shortness of breath and very weak and unable to talk. The EMT's thought that they were going to lose him a couple of times. Gail looked at the other doctors and said well we all know what to look for now don't we?

After going over all the labs with the doctors, Gail saw that Michael drank a glass of wine every night and has alway's said that everyone should, it's good for your heart. Maybe there's something to that. They had ordered another set of labs about an hour ago and they ordered them stat, so they schould be at the nurses station by now. All three doctors agreed to stay on as a group, and as a favor for Ray. Walking back to the ICU unit,Gail stopped in the gift shop and bought a small red bear with a gold cross around it's neck. Gail knew it was a little silly but, she loved bears and everyone should have at least one, especially while in the hospital. Gail walked back into the room and gave the bear to Christina, the bear and Gail both got a big hug. Gail knew the bear would lift someone's heart other than her own, even if only a little while.

Before giving Ray and his family the news she wanted to talk to Ray alone first. Gail called him out of the room and took him to the waiting room down the hall. Please sit down for a minute Ray, we need to discuss a few things before we talk to the rest of your family. "Ray have they told you anything about the lab work that was taken when your father was first brought in to the hospital?" Ray shook his head no that they were hoping to hear something now that Gail was there. Ray, are you and your family aware of the potassium chloried in your fathers system and how it got there? Again he just shook his head no. Gail asked Ray, "do you or your family know anyone who would want to hurt your father?" "Why would anyone want to hurt Pop?" I don't think that anyone has even said a cross word with him. Gail continued by saying, potassium chloride is what they use in lethal injections for executions Ray. Someone was very serious about trying to kill your father tonight.

Ray sat with his hands folded and just stared at the floor. He then whispered that he didn't know or had his brother and sisters, but there was something strange about his two Uncles being there, he hadn't seen them in years. Being his fathers younger brothers, they still lived in Sicily, and the last Ray knew they hadn't moved to the United States.

Gail walked up and asked for everyone to please leave the room while all three doctors could examine Michael. Everyone left the room and went down to the waiting room except for Michael's two brothers. Gail asked them to please wait outside and she would call them right back in after they were done.They would not budge or even act like they heard her at all. Well, okay then, on the exam Gail knew what she was looking for and soon found it, a little needle mark on the right side of Michael's neck, placed very carefully between the fold lines just below his right ear lobe. Someone had tried to kill Mr. Bertolli but was interrupted in the act and was only able to inject a small amount and thank God it missed his jugular vein, or he wouldn't have made it to the hospital. If this happened at home, who would have tried such a thing and was Christina the next victim before being caught? Gail needed to talk to Ray and get some answers. So much for a quiet evening at home and alone.

Chapter 6

Gail and both of the other doctors decided to wait to talk to Ray or his family of their findings, they would hold their hand until they had to, there were too many players in the game. Gail did get to talk to Dr. Mucci alone and asked him since he was Michael's PCP, if he would hold off telling them anything and he said that he agreed with her but, only for 24 hours, once all of the test results came back he was obligaited to give them his results. Mr. Bertolli was going to remain in ICU until then so they could keep an eye on him. hope that we get some good news tomorrow and gets it worked out of his system.

After telling everyone that Michael was stable, Gail asked everyone to please go home and get some rest. Roberto, Angelina and Maria all left and took their children home for the night. Christina, Joelina, Ray and the two uncles stayed. Gail would take Ray home with her to get his car at some time. Gail asked Joelina to come with her to get coffee for everyone, mainly to pry anything out of her since she came in right after it happend. While walking to the cafeteria, Gail asked Joelina about any changes around the house or store that she could think of. Nothing that I can think of said Joelina, but she would be watching more and be a little more alert to what's going on around at home and at the store. Joelina like Ray said that the only thing weird was that her uncles were their almost right behind Joelina when she got home. That was the only thing out of the ordinary that she could think of. They called 911, that's how quick they came into the house after herself, and it only took the ambulance driver about 2-3 minutes to get there and start working diligently on her father. Joelina was going to make up a basket of goods and take to the firehouse in the morning to thank them for being so prompt she said. "Who was there when this happened Gail asked Joelina?" My mother was the only one there, she was coming up from the basement with a basket of laundry when she heard the back door close. Once at the top she asked Michael who was just here and that's when he fell over off of the kitchen chair. Mamma was trying to pick him up when Joelina got there, she did see a gray car speeding down the street and she had to pull over or get hit by the crazy person driving the car.

While walking back to Michael's room, Gail saw the man in the long trench coat again, this time Gail asked him if she could help him with anything. He just walked out the door very fast and left. One more crazy person in this world thought Gail. Gail asked Joelina to go on in with the coffee and she would be right behind her, she needed to talk to the nurse. Gail asked Mary if she saw or knew the man in the trench coat. Mary said that she didn't know him, he was just at the desk asking her if Mr. Bertolli had passed away yet. When I told him that he was probably going to make it through, he started to panic and said that he needed to see him, himself. I told him that there were already too many people in the room, but she would go and get one of Michaels brothers to talk to him and when I turned around to say something to him that's when I saw you coming down the hall. Gail gave Mary a cup of coffee and then went back into the room. Gail decided not to say anything about the mystery man at least for know. After giving everyone coffee, Gail excused herself and went to find Dr. Mucci and Dr. Litzey. After talking to them they all agreed to having a 24 hour protection at the door to Mr. Bertolli's room. Gail called the police station and was transfered to a Captain Terry Lane, he said that he would send someone right away and they would continue every 12 hours, then they could switch from 7 a.m. to 7 p.m. Captain lane also told Gail that their house had been searched for any wrong doing so he hoped that they wouldn't be too upset, but we had to treat it as a crime scene, and no one was there once the ambulance took off, so we had to contain the scene and then locked up. I already have a man on his way to talk to family members. Gail told him what she knew form everyone else and that Mr. Bertolli's brothers would be able to talk with the officer on his way there now. Gail thanked him and then went to talk to Ray.

Gail walked in and pleaded for everyone to go home and get some rest. Christina finally agreed to go home with Joelina. Ray got his uncles to leave with him but they said only one at a time would go rest and then change places, that was the only way they would leave their brother. Vincent went first and Gail told Dominic that a police officer would be here very soon to talk to a family member, he just nodded his head. It was already 7 a.m. and Gail was very tired with no sleep herself.

Gail called her nurse Pat and asked her to reschedule her afternoon patients, she would do her rounds while she was at the hospital now and then come in to see her morning patients. Gail finally made it home by 1:30 and was ready for a shower and a bed, she turned her phone down so if it did ring it wouldn't startle her too much.

She had all calls going through her answering service. Dr Inlow would be covering for her today except for Mr. Bertolli she would take that call herself. She fixed her a bowl of cereal and some toast. After that she stepped into the shower then into bed. Home was an hour drive from the hospital but it was also so much quieter than town, away from the noise of St. Louis. Gail was trying to go to sleep but, the last 24 hours came rushing back to her mind. Did she really know Ray's family, or were there things hidden, and what about those Uncles Dominic and Vincent? The lab tests the look on Christina's face. What was really going on?

Chapter 7

Setting her alarm for 6 p.m. Gail lay down and tryed to get some sleep but, there was too much going on around her. She finally dozed off and sleep deeper than she thought she would. When the alarm went off she still didn't want to get up and leave her warm bed, but she did want to go back to the hospital and check on Mr. Bertolli. Gail dressed and tied her long strawberry blonde hair up into a clip. No one had called her so she was hoping for good news when she got there.

She left her house and went straight to the hospital. After parking her car, she thought she saw that man in the trench coat again by the slidding doors,but before she could get there he was gone. Gail made a mental note to talk to the police officer that was posted outside Mr. Bertolli's room about this man. Gail had just pushed the elevator button when the doors opened and Dominic Bertolli came running out of the door and headed for the outside doors. Gail stayed and watched him looking around the parking lot like he was looking for something or someone. He slowly walked back in and onto the elevator with Gail. "Mr. Bertolli, Gail said, are you going to let us know what's going on around here or not?" He remained silent as usual and got off of the elevator and back into Michael's room.

Gail walked up to the police officer and told him that she wanted to speak with him after she checked on her patient. He assured her that he would be there until 7 a.m. he was just starting his 12 hour shift. Gail told him it wouldn't be too long and she would be back, in the meantime she wanted to start with him and keep a log of who was on duty, their badge number, years on the force and their whole name and rank. The police officer assured Gail that there would be no problem with any of that. Gail just wanted everyone who came into Mr. Bertolli's room to be accounted for also. He went over to the desk and got a clip board from the lady there and said well, let's start with you and me, how does that sound? Gail laughed and signed her name and hospital badge number and told the nice young man thank you.

Gail walked into the room and Roberto and Dominic were the only ones there. Hello Roberto, were you able to get any rest? No, I layed there and let my body rest, but my mind would not let me sleep, so I came here to stay with Pop. Gail went over and took Michael's vitals again and they were better than before and his face swelling was going down, but he had yet to wake up. Maybe he was finally getting the rest he needed and never allowed him self to take because of the store. His coloring was much better than when she saw him last. Gail was starting to think that he will come out of this with no problem, he seemed on the road to recovery. When he wakes up, maybe he can tell us what happened and who would do this to him.

Christina was walking in as Gail was walking out. After getting them signed in, Gail took her hand and said, he looks better and his vitals are starting to respond to him being here and getting the rest he needs. "Are you sure, asked Christina?" Praise God said Joelina who came in with her mother. "Yes, much better said Gail". I don't know how to thank you for our family said Christina, but the Lord is with Michael also. "Will he come home soon asked Joelina?" Well we need for him to wake up before we can make any decisions, but he is on the road to recovery it seems. Roberto asked his mother to step outside and Gail walked out with them to fill in the chart, she stayed within ear shot of what they were saying. "Mama, when did Uncles Dominic and Vincient get here into town?" Christina said that they had called the night before last and that they would see us the next day. They got to the house right after your father fell over and they called 911 they came in right behind Joelina and I'm so thankful that they did, I was so scared Roberto. Everything will be fine now Mama, you'll see, you can't keep a man like Pop down for long and then he held his mother close. "Are you worried Roberto that something is not right asked Christina? No Mama, things are fine, Pop will wake up and tell us what happened, but Roberto was afraid everything wasn't right. Roberto knew that he would have to be careful about how he asked his Uncles questions. He remembered how it was when he spent a little over a year with them in Sicily. Yes, Roberto thought, very careful indeed.

Chapter 8

While Roberto and Christina talked for a while about the children, Gail went in to see her patient, Mr.Gary Kadell. He was just finishing his snack before bedtime, but was alway's up for a joke. Mr. Kadell was still fighting off some of the effects of time spent in Vietnam, it started as a yeast infection and turned into an STD (sexually transmitted disease) years ago, but now he was having problems again and didn't know why. Gary was also fighting Jungel Rot on his feet that a lot of men came back with. This time he also had a shoulder replacement that was also trying to get infected. Gail never asked questions about Vietnam, he clams up and turns his back to her, so she no longer brings it up. Gail could only cure what she could now. Gary started telling Gail a joke and he was laughing more than she was. "How long have you been telling these jokes of yours Gary?" I have never heard the same one twice in the four years that you have been my patient, asked Gail?" He replied, only about 40-50 years or so, but when are you going to marry me and that's no joke. "You work on getting better and then we'll talk, how does that sound Gail said". "Now that's a deal Doc.,I'll be out of hear in no time at all, so you get that wedding dress ready because I'm one hell of a dancer, and I think I could match you step by step." I may be gettting older, but I can still get it done. Just give me a few weeks to get this body in shape Sweet Pea, and I'm all yours. You just try and rest Gary and I'll be in tomorrow to check on you and your behavior laughed Gail. I'm on my best behavior Sweet Pea, see you tomorrow.

After seeing Mr. Kadell Gail went to get some coffee and ran into Ray, he had just came back with his Uncle Vincent so Roberto and Dominic could go get some rest. "I think Pop is looking a little better today, don't you Gail?" Indeed I do, lets walk and talk if that's okay with you? Yes, fine anything for my Princess. Ray, how well do you know your Uncles?" Ray replied that he hadn't seen them in a really long time, but there is something that they are not telling Roberto and myself and we are getting very perturbed by it."What do you mean Ray?" The only time they come to the States is when someone gets married or dies and an occational reunion, but most of them are held in Sicily. Mamma says that they will let it be known all in due time, but I have a bad feeling about something, I just don't know what it is yey, or even if I want to know. Gail had a bad feeling also, plus her stomach was a little upset, too much coffee for one thing.

Gail's beeper went off and it was Mary from ICU. They rushed back to the floor and were greeted with a big smile from Christina. "He is awake my son, come, look see." God has answered our prayers, thank you Lord. Gail walked up to the bed and and Dr. Mucci was also there taking another EKG. He's out of the woods it seems, said Dr. Mucci. What do you think Dr. McDougal? All she had to do was look at Michael starring at Christina with all the love in his heart, and she knew things would be fine.

"Have I been asleep long my dear, he asked Christina? Only enough to get you rested, something that you have been needing for a long time. "I love you so much Pappa, cried Joelina as Ray held her in his arms, then everyone was crying, even the "UNCLES" got a little misty, but no one was suppose to know. Standing at the foot of the bed Gail started thinking about her own mother and father, Elmer and Leah McDougal, so much in love, so little time. They had many years together and many stories to tell.

Gail remembered her mothers telling of the time when they were awakend at 2 a.m. with a fox or something in the chicken coop. Your father got out of bed, put on some boots and his hat, turned on the floodlights, grabbed his shotgun and went out the door,"no clothes". That should have scarred anything away out there said our mother. Well Gail's family owned a boxer whose name was Elvis, Gail's sister Ann had named him, a big Elvis Presley fan. Well it seemed that when her father got up to the chicken coop, Elvis stuck his cold nose up her fathers backside and he fired off the gun killing over half of the chickens. Gail's mother was furious. They were all up cleaning the chickens until daylight. No one was talking, just kept on picking feathers off of the chickens. Gail was glad she was still small or she would have had to help clean them and they did not smell good at all. It was a very, very long night.

Gail?, Gail?, are you alright? It was Ray, stating that Dr. Mucci had just asked her a question. I'm sorry, what did you say Dr. Mucci? I was just saying that if he is as good in the morning as he is now, that he may get to go home. That sounds wonderful, so I'll meet you in the morning around seven to do rounds? You bet said Dr. Mucci and I'll talk to Dr, Litzey and let him know also, I will see you all then, and then he was gone. Gail was still there when the police officers were changing shifts. Vincent and

Dominic were there checking his badge numbers and how long that he had been on the force. They seemed pleased by the mans answers. Whenthey went back into Michael's room, the police officer asked Gail if he could speak with her a moment. They walked a little ways from the room down to the nurses station. My name is Officer Dave Womack and Captain Lane asked for me to tell you to call him no matter what the time, day or night, but he needed her to call him. Gail thanked officer Womack and went back into the Room to get some people out of there and they all could use some rest, including herself.

Vincent and Dominic were to stay the night with their brother. Gail said her goodnights and then she and Ray left for the parking lot. As they were walking to Gail's car, Ray asked Gail when she was going to tell him what was not going on, and when was she going to tel him. "What do you mean Ray?" "My father almost lost his life and now he may be going home tomorrow?" And what about my uncles timely visit? "Please tell me something or I'm going to lose my mind." Gail took a moment before saying anything, she wanted to say it well so as Ray could understand, what she herself wasn't even sure of as of yet. But she would get to the bottom of it.

Chapter 9

Ray, your father had an attempt on his life, if your mother had not interrupted it at just the right moment, your father would be dead. Ray could only stop and stare at Gail with sullen eyes. "Who would ever want to kill my father?" He is the most loving man I know. He wouldn't even harm a fly and everyone he knows loves him. They started walking again to Gail's car, Ray would have to come with her because his car was still at her house in Illinois. Driving home both were silent, trying to think of who could have done this horrible thing and why. Gail looked over at Ray and her heart went out to him. "Ray, why don't you spend the night, I need to be back at the hospital at seven, but maybe you could sleep in for a while. We can both start the day off with a fresh mind and try to sort out all of this mess. Ray could only nod yes.

When they arrived home she let Ray have the shower first. While he was in the shower, Gail called Captain Lane. After only two rings he answered, it was already one thirty in the morning and he was still up waiting for her to call? Maybe someone else had a hard time sleeping too.

Dr. McDougal, how well do you know the Bertolli family, do you know a lot about them? I think we need to talk tomorrow if you can spare me a moment, I can meet you at your office or the hospital which ever is good for you. Gail had already cancelled all of her patients for tomorrrow with her office nurse Pat so she asked Captain Lane to meet her there at about two if that was good for him. "Yes that would be fine, it will give me some more time to gather up some more information before we speak." I hear that you are involved with Mr. Ray Bertolli?" We have a history Gail told him. If possible could you find out anything from Ray or his family members, or do you think they will clam up on you? Gail told him she would try and would see him at her office at two tomorrow afternoon, then she hung up. Gail wondered if he knew that Ray was with her now. Ray came out from the shower and asked Gail who she was talking to. Only checking my answering service about orders for the next day, she would stay on call for hospital and very sick patients, but the office would be closed otherwise. She gave the staff a day off also, she would need to catch up on some of her charts.

Come over here and sit next to me Ray, I need to ask you some questions. Ray walked over to her and sat down. "What's wrong Gail?" With everything that's been going on, do you believe that your uncles are here for more than a family visit?" Ray shook his head no, what I think is that something is going on in Sicily or about someone else here in the States and my poor innocent father almost lost his life over it. Gail was almost afraid to ask the next question but knew she had to. "Ray, is your family involved with the Mafia or some other mob family conflict that maybe your uncles could answer for him and the rest of his family?" Ray studied the rug on the living room floor and started to shake all over. "Ray, are you okay?" Please just try and stay calm until we find out anything. I know it's hard Raybut, try and stay with me Ray. Together we can work this out. "Do you really mean together Gail?" Gail knew then that she loved Ray and was truly "in" love with him, she kissed him and said yes Ray, I mean together, I love you so much. Oh babe I love you too, said Ray. Ray stood up and held his arms out for his love to step into and Gail didn't hesitate for one second. Ray began to kiss Gail all down her neck and shoulders, taking off layers of clothing as they made their way into the bedroom. Gail was dizzy with the love rising up inside her, yes she loved this man and it took half the night letting him know it. When the alarm went off they were still wrapped in each others arms, just how they fell asleep, they managed to get 3 hours of sleep. Gail wanted Ray to stay and get some more rest but, he was up and getting dressed already, He said he had some questions that needed to be answered and also had some questions of his own to ask, and he wanted them now. Ray went from being afraid to being very angry at his uncles. Gail went in to take a shower and when she came out dressed and ready to go to work, Ray had made some coffee and toast for her and had her bowl with the cereal in it, just neded to add the milk. He wanted them to start out as one this morning and for the rest of their lives. Gail just smiled and sat down to eat with the man she loved.

Chapter 10

Gail arrived a little late for the seven o'clock rounds. Dr. Mucci and Dr. Litzey were still waiting for her when she got to thr doctors lounge. "Well young lady, any luck as to what might have happened to Mr. Bertolli?" Gail responded with what she knew as fact, and told them of her meeting with Captain Lane this afternoon. Before they went out on rounds, they asked Gail to keep them updated and for her to be careful. "Yes and one more thing, you might have covered up that hickie before you got here, both doctors walked out just a laughing. Gail went over to her locker and opened it up to the mirror she had stuck to the inside door. Oh my, Gail never paid any attention to it when she was getting reasy this morning. Thank God she kept some bandaids in her pocket of her lab coat. She put it on her neck and smiled to herself, that was one war wound that she will always remember. Gail went out to see her patients then they all three would meet to go in to see Mr. Bertolli.

Gail went to see Mr. Kadell first and as usual he hade the housekeeper in stitches with a story about milking pigmy goats or some other insane storis that he always came up with. "Well Mr. Kadell, it seems as if you mat be ready to leave us by tomorrow, your shoulder is much better and your white count is getting back to normal. I still want you to take the antibiotics when you go home so that you don't start getting sick again alright? You do realize that you shoulder wont be the same as before, you will need to take it a little slow and do what the physical therapist tells you to do. "As long as I can reach out to you, and wrap you in my arms, I'll be happier than a stud jack rabbitt." I'll see you tomorrow and I might let you go home and into therapy. I"ll be right here waiting for you "Sweet pea". Gail walked out laughing and trying to remember when he first started calling her that. Mr. Kadell was one of a kind, and the world could use a few more Mr. Kadell's if you asked her. After seeing Mr. Hanson and Mrs. Youngblood, Gail was ready to see Ray's father. They all three arrived at the same time to go in to see Mr. Bertolli. "Nice bandage, did you burn yourself with the curling iron, said Dr. Mucci, then they all started laughing. Now stop Gail said, we are suppose to be professionals here. They all calmed down but with big grins on their faces. They all went in to see him and as like the day before both of his brothers were by Michaels side at the head of the bed. "How are you feeling today sir, Gail asked." I feel like being out of this bed, I have a store to run and a wife to tell me how to do it he laughed." Mr. Bertolli, said Dr. Mucci, your bloodwork this morning is a lot better than yesterday, do you remember what happened at home before you came to the hospital?" Dominic bent down and whispered something in Michael's ear, then he replied that he couldn't remember anything, but would let us kbow if he recall's anything. We could tell that we were not going to get anything out of him as long as his brothers were there. Dr. Mucci signed his release form and told him to call the office for an appointment next week, no excuses, and to have his labwork done the day before his appointment. Christina and Joelina were walking in as the doctors were walking out. Gail stopped to talk to them. "Is my father coming home today, asked Joelina?" Yes, Gail told them, he can go home just as soon as he eats breakfast and can keep it down. Gail told them that she would come to see him in the next few days to check up on him.

Christina could not have hugged Gail any tighter, you are a wonderful woman and doctor and Ray is a very lucky man to have you. God has blessed all of us when he brought all of you into my life also Gail said. I will see you tomorrow, and with that all three doctors left the room. Once outside the room Dr. Litzey told Gail that he would cover for her if she needed him to and Dr. Mucci said the same. I'm covered right now, I cancelled my office today, but thank you both for the kind jesture. Gail, said Dr. Mucci, please be very careful and watch your surroundings, you never know, and try and find out what happened, it would look better in my chart if I knew anything. Gail told them both that she would try and get some answers for them and herself. Dr. Litzey turned around and said, and watch out for those rouge curling irons, then down the hall the two went with Gail still laughing at the nurses desk. Ray was coming down the hall when Gail was still at the nurses station finishing charts. Ray walked up and kissed her and thanked her for taking care of his family, then another rib crushing hug. Ray told her that when they got their father home, they were all going to get some answers to unanswered questions. Ray had asked Roberto to meet him at the hospital, but he was unable to, so he was going to meet with all of them at their parents house this afternoon. Gail can I see you tonight after we talk to our uncles? I have some shopping to do then I'm going to my office and get some charting done, call me and maybe we can meet there before i go back home for the night.

Gail got her shopping done in record time, she hated shopping, that's why she alway's catalog shopped for the holidays. When she got to her office she could hear the phone ringing from outside the door. She got the door unlocked and in but, wasn't fast enough. It was her back line also, well maybe they would try again. Gail had givin her staff the day off with pay and the answering service would field the calls to her for any emergency. The phone rang again and this time she got it. It was Captain Lane and asked if they were still on for two o'clock. Yes we are, or he could come over now if he wanted to. Captain Lane said that he had one more thing to take care of but, he would be right over. Gail hung up and started towards her back ofice when she thought she heard the door knob rattle. She went up and peeked out the peep hole in the door but no one was there. She decided to go ahead and keep the door locked until Captain Lane got there. She was starting to feel sick to her stomach again, what if someone was after her, could that be possible due to her seeing Ray? Now she really felt sick.

Chapter 11

Captain Lane was there in forty-five minutes and he knocked on the door. Gail looked out before opening the door to let anyone in she had spooked herself and was very nervous now. "Could you please show me your badge and identifacation? Captain Lane showed her what she needed. I'm sorry but someone has been rattleing my door knob and when I look out, no ones there, she told him as she let him in. Please, come in and have a seat, would you like something to drink? I'm afraid I only have orange juice or a bottle of water. Water would be fine he said. Gail came back with two bottles of water and gave him his. "Have you heard anything from the Bertolli family yet, Dr. McDougal?" Please call me Gail, and nothing as of yet, but I'm suppose to meet with Ray tonight after a family meeting at his parents house. "What do you think happened to Mr. Bertolli Gail?" And, please call me Terry, I have a feeling that we will be seeing more of each other than we like. "I know what happened to him, he was almost murdered." Terry looked at her but, didn't looked surprised to hear that. "What exactly did you find Gail?" She began to tell him what she knew to be true, and what Mrs. Bertolli told her about how she thought she heard someone run out the back door when she was bringing up the laundry. So, you were able to see the needle mark in his neck, like officer Womack told me? Yes as did Doctor's Mucci and Litzey. We all wrote it down in our charts and and gave a copy to the police officer that was there this morning, it's probably on your desk as we speak. I had only give it to him after we all signed off on it when we released Mr. Bertolli this morning around 11:30. Dr. Mucci is his Primary Care Physician, so he signed it as an attempted murder, and also informed his family about it. "If you don't mind Terry, what do you know about the Bertolli family?" "Were you able to find anything out on your own?" Tery took a few minutes to get his thoughts together, then he preceded to tell Gail what he knew.

The Bertolli's were all originally from Sicily, except Michael and Christina's children, they were born here in the United States. Michael, Dominic and Vincent are the children of Maximillion (Max) and Olivia Bertolli. Max was part of the Sicily Mafia and couldn't get out, he tried but was met with horrible consequences. As Olivia was coming back from a day of shopping, she was run off the road, then killed by several gunmen. The next afternoon black roses arrived at their home, no note, no anything, but they knew it was from one of the other Mafia Don's. Max tried to send all of his sons to the States so they could have a normal life away from it all. Only Michael would leave because Christina was five months pregnant with Roberto. Vincent and Dominic were still young boys and not yet married, they vowed to repay the price of their mothers death.

Gail was trying to take all of this in slowly, but was still trying to comprehend what all of this is leading up to. Terry went on; Michael and Christina moved here to St.Louis soon after arriving in the States. Michael refused to have anything to due with payback's, guns or anythingelde that could harm his family. "Wait a minute Terry, are you telling me that someone from the Sicily Mafia wants to harm Michael after all these years?" Michael was never involved in it, he left that all behind so his family could grow up with no fear for their lives. "What happened to all of that?" Who would want to hurt him and his family now. Terry stood up and walked over to the glass sliding door out onto her balcony, Gail was up on the third floor. I don't know a whole lot more than that, except that their mothers life was avenged about six weeks ago. They lay back for years and let the Mafia think that they had nothing to worry about. "Could you excuse me, I need to use your restroom?" Yes, of course, it's the third door passed the chart room to your left.

Gail was trying to take all of this in when Terry returned. So you think that's the reason Dominic and Vincent showed up out of the blue, said Gail? Yes, but not much more. Talk to Ray and see what his family has to say on this, and if anything, let me know. Terry said, I don't need anymore gangs, mobsters or anything else here in St. Louis. Why just last night, a woman was gunned down in Steak'n'Shake over a drug deal gone bad. Some stupid son of a bitch walked in and just started shooting, killing an innocent 20 year old girl in the process. The whole world is a shit hole and we are about to be flushed down with it. "Sorry for my language Gail, but sometimes we all have to vent, and blow off some steam. "Have you seen anyone or anything strange going on around you?" Gail then told him about the man in the trench coat at the hospital, what he said to Mary at the nurses station, and someone rattleing her doornob just before he arrived at her office.

Gail please be careful, and keep an eye out for anything out of thr norm. Gail said that she would and got up to walk Terry to the door. Now, lock this door behind me, and if need be when you leave and you don't feel safe leaving alone, call me and I'll send a sqaud car over to take you to your car and make sure you get home alright. And with that he was gone. Gail double checked all the doors and windows, who knew, someone might swing themselves over the roof tops to the balcony, she would take extra care from noe on.

Chapter 12

Gail set in her office and just starred out the window. How well did she know Ray and his family; or for that matter everyone she knew. Gail fell asleep in her office chair, still trying to figure out the whole world in general. She knew that she wouldn't have an answer to everything in this world, but she would still keep on trying, maybe that's how people got by day to day... The phone rang and almost scarred Gail right out of her chair. Hello? "Gail is that you, it's me Ray, are you okay?" Yes, I was just dozing in my chair, where are you? I'm at Mom and Pop's. We have talked all afternoon and I'm very afraid for my family, even for you because you are involved with me. "What are you saying Ray?" Please baby, can you come here or should I come over to your office? Until everything is settled and sorted out maybe you schould come here Ray. Ray told Gail that he would take a cab to her office in case anyone was watching for his vehicle, it was at his house he had rode over to his parents house with Roberto. Gail told Ray that she was going to order a pizza and he could pick up some non-alcohol drinks. Ray said that he would see her in a few minutes and then hung up.

Gail sat in shock almost, wondering about what happened and what was said at Ray's parents house this afternoon. Why would they all be in danger and most of all herself, all of the time she and Ray have been seeing each other she never felt in danger. Maybe some things were blown out of perportion, she could only hope. Gail called in her pizza order and then started working on her charts. While she was waiting he called her good friend Rosie Galore, after four rings she picked up. Hello stranger, how are things in the computor world? "Gail, how are you?" It's so funny I was just thinking of calling you, what's up? Well, I was just thinking maybe we can get together this Sunday for a drink and some good conversation. This Sunday isn't good for me, what about next Sunday afternoon at our favorite watering hole The Do Drop Inn. That sounds perfect and you know that Bones has that bucket o' beer special and taco's 2 for a dollar. Well count me in sister at around two o'clock, that would br great. I'll see you then. At the same time we alway's say, 'I LOVE YOU GIRL'! Then we hang up. Rosie's husband doesn't like for her to go anywhere without him tagging along, he is a real piece of shit. He doesn't work, Rosie works two jobs and she deserves some time to herself. Rosie's a very smart woman except when it comes to him.

Gail was locking everything up when she heard the elevator doors open, she went over to the door and looked out thinking it was Ray, but saw no one.She went to the kitchen to get some paper plates and napkins when she heard someone at the door. "I'll be right there, she hollered thinking it was the pizza man; she went to get her purse. When she got to the door and looked out, the pizza man was just coming out of the elevator. "Who was the person who was keeping on trying her door?" Gail opened the door for the delivery man and she asked him if he saw anyone at her door when he got off of the elevator, but he said he never saw anyone, but someone had just took the stairs, he heard the door close. Thank you so much. No problem enjoy your pizza. When the elevator doors opened, it was Ray, he stepped out and tipped the pizza man again. Thank you very much sir, have a good evening.

Ray walked in and kissed Gail hello, they walked in and locked all the doors behind them. Before we talk Ray, I need to eat something, i havn't eaten since this morning and if I don't I'm going to have a huge headache. Ray had also not eatin so he was glad to be eating also. Ray brought some soft drinks and juice, and two cups of ice. As they ate Ray stared at Gail the whole time, what if he lost her over this or worse, what if something happened to her because of his family. After eating and cleaning up, Gail felt like she was going to throw it all back up. Her nerves couldn't take much more. She sat in the kitchen again until she felt like standing again. Gail walked down the hall to the waiting room where Ray was seated, it was everything going on around her that was keeping her nerves on edge. Gail went over by Ray so they could talk. I don't even know where to start Gail, I know this is all of a sudden but, it is for me also. I fear for all of us, and I don't even know what to watch out for. Just start from the beginning Ray, and we can try and understand it together. Have I told you how much I love you today, said Ray. Yes, and you also left your calling card. Ray looked at Gail confused until she pulled her hair back and took off the bandaid. All at once they both started laughing, I promise I didn't know that I did that, it must have been that spell you put me under lastnight. Whatever it was it was perfect said Gail. they held on to each other while they talked. Ray started with what happend to his grandmother and brought her all the way up until now. His whole family and Gail was in danger if she chose to stay with Ray. Gail turned and looked at him and said remember, together, as long as we have each other we can face anything. "Then you'll stay with me knowing the danger it may bring?" I don't ever want to lose you Ray, not for any reason, so it's us together facing anything, alright? Ray grabbed Gail and held her so close and Gail just melted in his arms like a baseball fits perfectly into the glove.

Ray started to tell her about his grandfather that he never really knew and had only met once at Angelina's wedding, that was the first and last that he even saw him. Gail could only imagine what it must have been like for Vincent and Dominic growing up with all of that, it seemed to make her feel a little sorry for them, and could understand why they wanted to protect their brother like they did. It sounded like a movie, did these things really go on these day's? It's 2010 for God's sake, why isn't these things on the news anymore? All she ever saw was the gangs, mostly kids wanting to play the big man. God help those gangs if the Mafia started back up here as it wa in the early 1900's. Gail, Pop says thathe wil kep on seeing Dr. Mucci, but he doesn't want to put you in anymore danger than you are now, he said he will sign a records release form for you to keep up on his records for all of us. Ray, you tell your father that wild horses can't keep me away and they are stuck with me and so are you. Ray pulled her gently to him and kissed her so softly and then with urgency and it pulled them both back into the firepit of love. Have you ever had sex in your office before Ray asked Gail? Until right this moment no, thank got we have carpet and good housekeepers as she pulled Ray to the floor.

Gail and Ray talked for two solid hours after getting up off of the floor and straighting themselves up. Ray, does your uncles know who it is for sure that's trying to harm your family? No one for sure, but whomever it is they have to have family or connections here in St. Louis, that is why my uncles have come here, they to have contact's here and will be using them to find out who it is. They will find out, of this I have no doubt, and there will be no mercy if anyone from my family or yourself is hurt in this process. Just to be safe, I took a taxicab to a small deli store where I bought our drinks, I paid the driver to sit outside for ten minutes and then leave. In the meantime I crabbed another taxi and went out the backdoor to here. I looked around when I got here but never saw anyone or anything before I came into the building. As they got ready to go Gail hugged Ray and said please don't take any chances and alway's look around you at all times. Ray walked Gail down to her car and then he hailed a cab just after that, eyes watching them go.

Chapter 13

Captain Lane called into the station and asked to talk to officer Nichols who has been on the force with Terry for about 26 years. Bob, did anyone pick up any prints or anything suspicious at the Bertolli household a couple of nights ago? We dusted for fingerprints and searched for foot prints, broken branches, anything that we could beleive that it might be a break-in, but got no other prints than the family members. "Oh, take that back, we did find the cap to a syringe of a small insulin needle. When we asked about it we were told that one of their grandchildren had adolescent diabetes. Well how long was that cap there, and when was the last time that the child had been to the house and had to take an injection? We also need to find out if anyone else in their family or friends has diabetes or not. "Did we miss anything or is there something your not telling me asked Bob?" Terry said , you know me just trying to tie everything up with abig red bow. Bob, yes Terry, I still want around the clock watch on Michael Betolli's house. "What's going on Terry?" Just a hunch,but lets all keep on our toes, his brothers showed up from Sicily just moments before Michaels trip to the hospital. They were already here, flew in the day before. Dr. McDougal is suppose to help me find out anything that she can and let me know. Those two Dominic and Vincent Bertolli, Bob are the real deal, they have Sicilian Mafia written all over them, so we need to be very careful. Also, did an officer drop off some papers for me from the hospital, the one that sat outside Mr. Bertolli's room? Yeah, their here have been for a while, you probably would have seen them if you would ever clean up your desk. Oh yeah, real funny, haha. Bob, keep this under your hat for now until we can paste it all together. You got it Boss, see you soon. Captain Lane could smell something wrong, but he still needed a lot more information from over the ocean, he still had some contacts that he had met after the September 11, tragedy. He would also try the Internet, it was crazy what some people put on there these day's.

Chapter 14

Michael Bertolli sat and held his loving wife while she cried, he could only stare at his brothers Dominic andVincent, their heads held down. "Dominic, after all these years, you and Vincent have brought all of this down on my family?" We left our country to have a better life than we would of had if we had stayed, a safer life, my family is not involved in any of this! Vincent raised his head to his brother and said, "Do you think that we are responsible for this?" We did what we had to do, we waited, never married, sacrificing our lives for our mothers honor. Papa understood that you had to leave and move here for the sake of your family, but at the same time he needed Dominic and myself to help him through those last few years of his life. "As you know Michael, two more attempts were made on our father as he still tried to find a way out for us all. He died feeling like he failed us all, yes even you Michael. "Michael, whether you like it or not your name is also Bertolli, are you ashamed of your name?" "No, I'm very proud to be a Bertolli,

But I haven't angered anyone for them to do this to me." "Do you think our mother angered anyone, only to have her killed for nothing?" You didn't have to do anything, whomever is doing this now, knows us all, everyone of us, that's why we think it's family or friend related.

"We avenged our parents as we were left with no other option." " Revenge is a dish best served cold, and we waited years for them to eat it." "I will not apoligize for what had to be done." I am however sorry that it has brought danger to your loved ones. We will be here until this threat is ended. We don't know who it is or why they came after you, or how they even knew where you lived. What we do know is that there was someone in your home and also tried to see you in the hospital. He is the one who tried to kill you. Thank you Christina for coming to our brothers rescue, words are not enough. "You are welcome to stay in our home while you are here said Christina, but understand this; if any of my family members are hurt or killed, I will hold you both responsible." She then got up and went into the kitchen to make dinner for everyone.

Joelina was sitting the table for five, Papa,Mama,Dominic, Vincent and herself. Everyone else had left for the comforts of their own homes, still confused. As Jolina set the table, Joelina looked at her uncles and said, "while you are in my fathers house I will respect you, but if something happens to my parents or family, then I will become the hunter, even if you are the prey." Do I make myself clear? Her uncles nodded to her and said, now you know how we felt about our parents, and that is good that you feel that way, it means that your family comes first. Joelina starred at both of them and then left for the kitchen. "She is a true Bertolli, it is in her eyes and her blood, I pray that she will be careful, said Dominic." We will follow our brothers rules while in his house, but our rules everywhere else. Dinner was very quiet and so was the rest of the evening.

While getting ready for bed Vincent and Dominic made sure everything was locked up tighter than a drum. When looking out the window, Vincent saw that the police were still watching over their brother Michael. Strange thought Vincent, I alway's try to avoid the law, but now it felt good to have more on thier side. Dominic would take the first shift while Vincent got some sleep, they would change evey four hours, they knew that it could still be dangerous to let their guard down. They would make sure that nothing happened to their dearest and oldest brother again. They did have some leads into who was involved, but it would get very bad before it got better, The two brothers prayed they had the right contacts.

Chapter 15

Gail drove on home to Hickory Grove and pulled into the garage and locked everything up. She watched all the way home and even took a couple of different roads to make sure no one was following her. She was glad that she lived in a small town like Hickory Grove, small town, small problems, well most of the time. They had crime in their town like others, but not as bad as bad, at least she hoped not. She called Ray to let him know that she made it home, then Gail fixed herself a hot cup of tea and went upstairs to bed, after rechecking all the doors and windows again. After a shower and settleing into bed it took Gail a little while to go to sleep, trufully it took about ten minutes, but felt like hours. She knew that she was sleep deprived the last couple of days. Her alarm clock was set for seven, and she had a full day at the office, some patients double booked due to rescheduling from the last few day's.

Ray also got home and locked everything up. He went up to take a shower and straight to bed, he had a party tomorrow night and still had to finish the ice carving. He couldn't stop thinking about Gail and hoping he wouldn't lose her over his family's problems. He got back up and double checked his doors and windows one last time. Gail had called and let him know that she was home and locked up, he felt that he could sleep knowing that for now she was alright. "Please Lord, don't let anyone hurt my family or the woman I love." And with that he fell asleep also.

Officers Marshall and Womack were assigned to watch the Bertolli house from 7 p.m. to 7 a.m. Day shift would be Cunningham and Chappel, twelve hour shifts until they recieved new instructions. While they were on watch, Marshall was in the front seat and Womack was in the back facing each other so that they had veiws on both sides of the street. Thank goodness for Womacks wife, she alway's made sure that they had plenty of snacks and coffee to keep them awake for 12 hours.

As they were keeping a watchful eye out, a car was slowly coming down the street, as it got closer it almost came to a stop. Marshall took his gun from his belt and slowly rose to see who it was. Two men in a 1998 dark charcol grey Grand Am, and both of them had on sunglasses, at night? Before Womack could sit up to get a licence plate number, they sped away in a flash. They could not leave their post but, did call it in for patrol to try and get them. When they radioed back, they said that they never saw them or any car that fit that discription. Discouraged, Marshall and Womack returned to their places in the car. Womack asked Marshall, why do people were sunglasses at night? What did it do to help them watch the road at night? Marshall wasn't sure but he would ask Captain Lane in the morning to see if there was some kind of law for it or not. Maybe we will get the chance to pull them over and ask them next time said Womack, Let's talk about something that will keep me awake.

Chapter 16

Watching from the front door, Dominic saw the car also and was almost sure of who was in it. He would let Vincent know about it when he wakes up to change shifts. Dominic went over to get him a cup of coffee when Michael came out and asked for a cup also, said he couldn't sleep. Christina fell asleep as soon as she got into bed, it's been hard on her these last few day's. Sit down Dominic, I want to know it all, so sit here and tell me. I have the right to know. After looking out the windows and doors again Dominic sat down with his brother. It seems that we have made a mess of things for you and your family and for that I am truly sorry and saddened by it. Our father died feeling as if no justice was done for our mother. You should have seen the way he would just sit around and look at nothing, starring at the walls, out the window, like a lost sheep Michael. I know that you had to come here to the States for your family's sake, but it left Vincent and myself to get our fathers justice.

"Why did you have to do anything?" You could have moved here when Papa died, you had a choice, said Michael. No! We did not have a choice Michael, you should have been there to see, and then you would have known that we didn't. "Our father lost his soulmate when Mama was killed and he never recovered" He would never leave the house unless we forced him to. Nothing held any joy for him, he gave up careing about anything, the house, the olive orchard, even his family. He never wrote those letters to you Michael, we did, Vincent and I, we did it so we could stay in touch with you here.

"Do you know what it's like to see a family member tied up to a tree then riddled with bullets?" No, you don't do you? Michael said, keep your voice down, you will wake up Christina or worse Joelina, she's a hard ass just like Max. I'm sorry I will try, but Michael you have to understand that Vincent and I saw it all, we were only 14 and 15 when you left us, and I hold no grudge for that, but you must understand that it was not easy for us. Dominic took a long breath and then continued. I was dating a very nice and very beautiful woman Michael; her name was Veronica, a real beauty a lot like your Christina. We were coming home from having dinner out, she picked me up in town and then drove me home. When she left she was run off of the road like Mama, only she didn't die. She tried to get away from them but, there was three of them, they took turns rapeing and beating her. I called and tried to see her while she was in the hospital and when she came home, but I was shot down and told to never call or see their daughter again. Some say it was the Corondo brothers, but no one would talk. My heart was broken.

Not only that Michael but, they burned down one third of of our olive trees. "Do you know how much that hurt Papa?" He really went down hill after that. Vincent and I are here for one reason only; to watch over you and your family like we did Papa before he passed on.

We waited a year Michael, before we avenged our parents, and we were not sloppy about it. The Gianti family did not suspect us of what we had done; that is until someone told them that it was Vincent and I. The family said that they believed us and we shook hands with Mr. Gianti. Someone in our family Michael, is spreading bad rumors of things we have never done, but are being blamed for. We avenged Mama's death the same way that they took her away from us, only we didn't take someone's mother, we took the Grandfather that put out the hit on our mother. That is the whole story Michael, I swear on our parents graves, nothing else. Now Mama and Papa are together again. We are being blamed for the three hit's of the Corondo boy's murders, but it was not us. Michael asked Dominic," Who do you think killed them and how did they die?" I"m not sure Michael, but Veronica had four very large brothers and they found the Corondo brothers, hanging from a tree castrated, I feel that justice was done, and I do feel better, but it was not Vincent or myself.

We didn't mean for you and your family to go through this, but like I said, we think that it's someone in our family, a cousin, a spouse we just don't know yet. I'm not sure how they found you and your family, but from now on we all must be very careful and keep a watchful eye. Our obligation is to you and your family first and foremost.

Michael,speaking of friends, this Doctor friend of Ray's, she sure is a great woman to have around, the way she took care of you, and it was her who tipped us off about the man in the trench coat that was asking about you at the hospital. I tried to catch up with him but he was gone already. She is also a very good looking woman, Ray will have his hands full with this one. I"m sorry that we gave her such a hard time, but you are our first obligation Michael. Vincent and I will take turns going back and forth to the store with you. We will make sure that we don't set a pattern for anyone, we have no choice we must stick together. Michael nodded and said, maybe I should have stayed with Papa, and not put such a burden on you and Vincent. "No Michael, you were right in leaving, what if it was Christina, instead of Veronica?" You would have wanted revenge too and you know it. Again Michael nodded. "well we are a force to be reckoned with, hey Dominic?" Who is watching the buisness while you and Vincent are away? Damitrius, he is our manager in the fields and the house staff will take care of that. We will keep in touch with them each day.

Michael got up and hugged his brother and thanked him for letting him in on all that they have been through. "Dont worry Dominic, your big brother won't go down without a fight, and I pray that you are wrong about it being a family member, if it is so, we will not make it easy on them. "What is it they alway's say?" Keep your family close and your enemy's closer, we will see. Goodnight Dominic, I love you. With tears in his eyes, Dominic said goodnight also. Outside Marshall and Womack stayed vigilant, but nothing out of the ordinary went on the rest of the night, or for the rest of the week for that matter.

Chapter 17

After almost a week Gail finally got a good nights sleep, and was at the office at 7:45 a.m. She would start her patients at nine so she had a little time to work on some charts. She greeted the staff when they came in all chipper from having an extra day off, with pay. Gail had a good staff and wanted to keep them, especially Pat, her nurse and office manager. She was glad to have her after the last one that she had who tried to rob her blind and alway's had the staff in jitters all day long. Pat found out later just how bad that her old manager (Cathy) had stolen and told lies on everyone else in the office, she had no choice but to let her go. Now everyone is glad to come to work each day, knowing that their not going to get their heads torn off. Pat had a saying on the wall above the time clock that say's; "Do you ever notice how much happier the people who are late are, then the ones who are waiting on them?" That bell does ring true, and it does help keep people on time. Gail was just taking a short lunch break, when Ray called her.

Hey, how was last night? Did you get any sleep? Gail told him that she had, and asked him how his night went. I finally got seven hours of sleep, He needed it before the big party that he had tonight. Gail, I'm working out of the Ritz Carlton in Clayton Mo. where we first met. "Hey Babe, why don't you come down to the Ritz when your finished, and spend some time with me after you get out of there tonight?" Gail replied that she had to do rounds at the hospital because she didn't do them this morning. "I'll try after that if thats okay? Baby you know that it's okay with me. I'll be here late and I'll have my staff take everything back to my wharehouse for me, I have a great bunch of college kids working for me for a while when I have the large parties like tonight. Adam and Russell are the best and that's why I keep them fulltime jobs, they have dorm rooms at SLU (St. Louis Universary) so they don't have far to go from the wharehouse.

If I get done early I'll come by and have a drink with you and wind down, is that okay? Sure Babe, but call me one way or the other so I don't worry about you. We will just play it by ear until later and I'll know more then, and then she went back too seeing patients.

Gail was able to leave the office by seven, she worked on more of her charts while she could, it's a never ending battle, soon they would go paperless and it would be so much nicer in the long run. She headed over to the hospital all the while keeping an eye out for anything strange. Gail got to the nurses desk and Margie was on duty, and gave Gail the charts she needed. Margie was out of work for a little over a year fighting throat cancer, radiation, chemotherapy treatments, but no one fought harder than Margie. She won that battle and has been cancer free now for over five years, all in all a wonderful person.

Gail went in to see Mrs. Youngblood first. Hello Sherry how are you doing this evening? I just want to go home Dr McDougal, I think I'm doing alright. Well, let's have a listen to your chest and back for a moment. Gail took out her stethoscope and listened, it still sounded bad. I'm sorry Sherry but, I think you need a couple more days here and give those antibiotics a chance to do their work, you are still very congested. I'm going to have them come in every four hours with breathing treatment's for you and I want you to really take in long and deep breaths. I know that it makes you cough a lot, but you need to get that broke up in there. I'll see you in the morning then we'll see how much improvement you have, deal? Okay Doctor whatever you say. Well thank you Sherry, for not giving me any trouble about it, it's nice when my patients heed my advise. You get some rest tonight if you can, and I'll see you later, goodnight Sherry.

Next was Mr. Hanson, he was dozing when she entered the room. "Mr. Hanson, how are you feeling this evening?" Oh, I guess a little better, time will tell. Gail glanced at his chart and looked at his vitals for the day. She took his blood pressure herself and it was 200/110 and his pulse rate was 122. "Well, it looks like I need to change your medications. I"M taking you off of Cozar and putting you on Hyzaar 100/25 and put you on Verapamil 240mg. for your high pulse rate'. I'm also going to have the nurse give you a 0.1mg of Clonidine. Let's see how that works overnight and go from there. Well you know more about it than I do Doc, so do what you have to for me to get rid of this headache. I'll see you in the morning then, try and get some rest, Goodnight Mr. Hanson.

Next on the list was Ms. Boden; she was never in a good mood, if Gail said it was day, Cynthia would say it was night. No wonder her last PCP had dismissed her from his practice. She was alway's treating the hospital and office staff like crap. "How are you doing Ms. Boden?" "Why wern't you here this morning, did you take the day off or something?" I had to lay here all day and wait for you to show up. Now, Ms. Boden, where would you go said Gail, trying to be pleasent to her, you just had a five way bypass so you'll be here for at least three more days, and no I did not take the day off, I have been sleep deprived and finally got caught up on my sleep.Cynthia said, "I don't want to hear about your personal problems, how's my heart?" Gail took a listen and it was ticking like it should now, as opposed to before your surgery. Gail told her to have a good nights sleep and she would see her in the morning.

Gail walked back to the nurse's desk and asked Margie, Is Ms. Boden cranky like this all the time? "Oh, you missed this morning's excitment said Margie, she threw her food tray at one of our candy stripper's and almost scarred her to death." Gail said that she would have a talk with her in the morning, and for the staff to write down anything else that she say's or does. I may have to dismiss her from my practice, said Gail, everyone needs to be respected and she had better change her tune or she will go, it's that simple.

Chapter 18

Back at the Bertolli household, Roberta and Lucinda came over for dinner with their children. The two uncles got a chance to play with the children, while Lucinda helped Christina in the kitchen. Roberto was having a chat with his father about work. Papa, I think that you are going back to work too soon, and also will you be safe there? I will be fine Roberto, my brothers never leave my side, and they won't as long as there is a thraet out there for me. Roberto, we will make sure that your father is protected, you can be sure of that, said Dominic. Christine came out of the kitchen and asked Roberto to please get the booster seat for Lucas, so he can sit next to his Nana.

Lucinda came through the door and had a very large pan of lasagna with her, ah" Christina's specialty, and it smelled wonderfull. Everyone sat down to eat and Michael said, which one of you wants to say the prayer for this lovely food? It surprised everyone when Vincent said that it would be his honor. They all bowed their heads even little Lucus. "Our heavenly father, we thank you for this food, the roof above us and for this family." Help us remember that a family is for growing up in, for going away from and coming back to. It is for loving concern, for helping others through happy times and sad. With your blessings this family will alway's be together in our hearts and in our memories, giving each of us strength to live our own lives, and to be our own person. We thank you Lord, and for the blessings of today. Amen. "Amen, said Lucus, grabbing his bread. Thank you Vincent, that was lovely said Christina.

Joelina was coming in the front door but held back from coming any closer, she wanted to hear that prayer also, and to her amazement, it touched her own heart. She walked on in and sat down to the table to eat with the rest of them."Well Lucinda, said Dominic, where is your brother at these day's? I believe his name is Sonny? Am I correct? Oh, her's here and there, I don't think that he will ever settle down and start a family, he has his own house on Mama and Papa's property, he says that it's close if Mama needs him. Mama pays all of his bills and gives him money to live on, he is just lazy and doesn't want to work. Mama needs her money to support herself. And no one in your house or family has diabetes, except for little Lucas here, asked Vincent? Yes, only Lucus, thank God. Doe's he never come and visit his neice and nephews? Only when it fits his needs, if he's here in the states. Dominic asked, and when was the last time that he has been to see you? Lucinda replied that it had been a long time at least a year or more maybe. He stay's in hotels in town when he is here, I think it's because all of the noise that the children make. Roberto looked over at his Uncle Dominic and rolled his eyes, he never got along with Sonny anyway, so he really didn't care where he stayed, and the feelings were mutual. How is your mother, Lucinda, since your father has passed away, asked Christina? She has her bad day's and and her good day's, but all in all I think that she is fine. She won't leave her little patch of heaven as she calls it. She say's that she wil die and lay next to Pappa and continue on to their 52nd wedding anniversary, come this December. Well, God bless her, said Vincent.

Not to change the subject, but how is the Zoo's lion tamer these day's, Roberto? "I love it Uncle Vincent, really love it" Don't get me wrong, it's a very dangerous job, you have to know what your limitations are and them to know your's, there are day's that I keep my distance, and you never turn your back to them, you back out away from them if you have to. The little cubs are cute, and so much fun, very playful. We have a new little cub, we call him "Solo" because he was the only cub to the mother lion. Speaking of which, do you have to work late tomorrow, asked Lucinda? No, not tomorrow, but maybe Friday, one of our Leopard's is going to have two kittens. Once she has them, I will sedate her only long enough to take her babies and weight them and make sure that they are okay, then return them to her before she comes out of it, Lucus here got to see Solo didn't you fella? Lucus just nodded his head and kept on eating.

Now what kind of medicene is Lucus on, asked Dominic? He get's one shot of Insulin a day, sometimes two if he sneaks in some candy, he knows that he has to watch, but only being five, we have to watch him all the time, don't we Lucus? replied Roberto. He only nodded again and kept on eating. "Where in the world doe's he put all of that food, asked Dominic?" I think it all goes to his feet because they are almost the same size as mine, said Lucinda laughing." Do you alway's have to carry his medications where ever you go, asked Vincent, and doesn't it have to be in a refridgerator?" We have a cold pack that fits right into his medication packet, and it is good for 48 hours, said Lucinda, and we alway's carry a couple of syringes with us also, said Roberto.

Papa, said Joelina, changing the subject, everyone has been asking about you at the store, and wondering when you will be coming back. "I'll be there tomorrow dear, the doctor said so." Mama, is this true, surely it is too soon for him to return so quick, asked Joelina?" Dr. Mucci say's that he is fit as a fiddle. "What does that mean, I never understood this, what does a fiddle do, it doesn't get sick or better or whatever, is that not a crazy saying?" Everyone laughed at Christia's joke. Vincent was sitting back taking mental notes, and every now and then would look over at Dominic and nod his head. Mama, I need to take some time off tomorrow to do errands, I'll do deliveries then also, is that alright? "Yes sweetheart, you deserve more time than you get anyway, you alway's work too much to cover up for me and Papa." You take all the time that you need, we will be fine, one of your uncles will be with us.

Joelina looked at her Uncle Vincent and asked him if he would like to go for a walk and he said that he would. It will give me a chance to smoke this new cigar in my coat pocket. "What about you Uncle Dominic, would you like to go also?" No little lady, I'm going to sit in this chair and go to sleep after stuffing myself with your mother's wonderful dinner." We all knew that wasn't going to happen, not with three small children running and screaming, and Lucinda telling them to be quiet. With that Joelina and Vincent went out the door and started down the sidewalk.

Chapter 19

Marshall and Womack were still on the duty list for the Bertolli house. Mark wondered why no one ever was with the youngest daughter Joelina, she came in and out at all hours of the day and night. Maybe she was a black belt or better and could whip someone a good ass kicking, he still worried about her though, even enough that he would sometimes follow her even when he wasn't on duty, he had no idea why. They watched Joelina and her uncle Vincent coming out like they were going for a stroll, maybe they wouldn't be out long, the girl didn't have a sweater on and it was chilly out tonight. Mark and Dave thought it strange that they would be so careless at a time like this, right out in the open. There still was no arrest or suspects in the attempt on Michael Bertolli's life, so they thought it too early for them to be out strolling down the streets at night unprotected. Or maybe they were, Vincent Bertolli may be packing a gun, but they were not going to pat him down, not now, they were told to stay they're position, and to alway's keep looking for any changes. For the past week everything has been going fine, with no upsets of any kind. They were already coming back from around the block and now she had her uncles coat drapped over her shoulders, well at least he's a gentleman anyway. "Hey Marshall, you want a Twinkie or a Ding Dong?" Womack, you are a Ding Dong, and yes, I'll have a Twinkie, thank you and Jennifer for picking some snacks up for us.

While out walking, Joelina asked her Uncle Vincent if someone truly tried to kill her father. "yes, they did, and what's worse is that we think it is a family member or related to a family member said Vincent." "But how can that be, Papa has never done harm to anyone in his life." I know, but we can't take any chances, we need to be very careful Joelina. I would not have come outside with you for a walk if those two police officers wern't there watching us the whole time, they seem like very fine young men, don't you think dear? I wouldn't know I barely remember they are there. Really, who is that girl who is alway's sitting in the bay window seat pretending to be reading when really she is watching to see if she could get a chance to see that Marshall one? Uncle Vincent that is not funny, but she looked up at him and smiled. Did you notice anyone in the store today, whom you haven't seen before asked Vincent? We alway's have new people in the store, we are right down town, and at lunch time it get's a little crazy, but now that you mention it, there was this creepy guy in today that had on a long trench coat, it was pretty warm out today, much too warm for that coat, said Joelina. "Did he come in and buy anything?" Yes, only a soda and a bag of chips, and he was still outside about a block down, when I closed up the store. From now on Joelina, write down on paper anything that you see that is strange, like how tall, color of hair, shoes, tattoos, and try to be alert, try and stop a problem before it get's started if that's possible for you. You are a true Bertolli Joelina.

"Okay then Uncle Vincent, since I have to do this for you, you and Uncle Dominic have to keep me informed of anything." I will not see my father murdered or anyone else, including you and Uncle Dominic, okay? "Do you want to shake on it?" Sure, but I would much rather have a hug and a kiss on the cheek from my loving neice. Joelina said, while hugging Vincent, you know there are times when I am not as loving, don't you? I can be very hard headed, Papa calls me little Max sometimes. "Am I really like my Grandfather?" Yes, you most certainly are, but that's a good thing. You can be proud of that name, here and in Sicily

Chapter 20

When Joelina and her Uncle Vincent went back into the house, Mark lay back with a sigh of relief. Why was he so worried about this Bertolli sister, she was just an assignment like many before wasn't she? Mark tried not to let Womack see him looking at her the way he did, but it was too late. Dave looked like the cat who just ate the canary, he just layed back and smiled at Mark. Mark knew that he would hear it sooner or later, but it was okay for him to just wait for it, so he just layed back and started looking around to see if anyone else saw them outside also.

Joelina and Vincent came back into the house just as the table was cleared, Michael and Dominic were playing Gin Rummy. Christina and Lucinda was finishing up the last of the dishes. Vincent started playing with the children along with Roberto and the children were winning. Christina and Lucinda came out from the kitchen and asked if anyone needed anything, all replied no so the ladies sat down to rest. Mama, could you make a list from the store, I have invited Maria and her family over for dinner tomorrow night, if that's alright? "Of course, of course said Christina, they need no invitation to come here for dinner, so yes, I will make a list and you can drop it off here when your out doing your errands." Please drop it off at the house before 3 o'clock so I can start cooking the minute I get home. That will leave you and Papa and which ever one of these are going with him tomorrow, as she pointed to Dominic and Vincent. That would be me said Vincent. Everyone looked at him because he was down there most of the day with Christina and Joelina, but that was fine. Dominic would be going but, they needn't know until tomorrow morning when they left the house.

Well everyone, I'm going up to bed, said Joelina. She went and kissed everybody goodnight, and for Roberto to be careful going home. When she bent down to kiss her Uncle Dominic, she whispered, "I am a true Bertolli" and no one will hurt my family. I am on board now with you and Uncle Vincent. Dominic looked over to Vincent and he just smiled and nodded his head yes, and with that she went upstairs to bed.Joelina would have to be very careful from now on, but now she had allies with her two uncles, and there were two police officers outside their door also. Joelina walked over and took a peek out of her window and could only make out a ballcap in the back seat. While undressing, it dawned on her that if she could see them then they could also see her. She hurried and pulled the shades, took a shower and went to bed.

"Hey Womack, did you know that the youngest daughters room is right in my sight and the shades are up?" Before Womack could get turned around, the shades came down. "Why couldn't you have said something before man, I could have used a little excitment tonight." I'm getting bored sitting here night after night, and nothing happens. "You're the married man, so I get to look, not you. We are here to catch the bad guys remember? Womack looked up and down the street while he was up in the seat. Only the same cars as every night While Womack was checking out the streets, Marshall was thinking about Joelina, my but she was beautiful, if he was ever lucky enough to get the chance to, he would like to ask her out to dinner. Why would she ever want to go out with an Irish and Greek Policeman? Maybe when this was all over, a man can dream can't he! They both went back to their word games, since no one or anything was moving around them. Womack hated playing any kind of trivia with Marshall, when Mark was in the Marine corp. the men in his plattoon called him

Mr. Jephardy, not one to blow his own horn ,but he was a very smart person, and just one dinner date with Joelina would make him very lucky indeed. Maybe he should go to the store and introduce himself to her when it was all over. He would make sure that nothing happened to her or her family, he just needed to get the courage to ask her out. Mark could not get Joelina out of his head, oh well, back to the crosswords.

Chapter 21

Gail decided she would go to the Ritz Carlton and see Ray. She alway's kept different clothes at the office, for different occasions. She washed up and put a lovely powdered blue dress on, it really made her blue eyes sparkle. She let her hair fall down her back, it was up all day, so she was glad to let it down, a little makeup and she was ready. She called Ray and told him that she was coming. When she was ready to go, she peeked out the hole and no one was there, she opened her door and made a dash for the elevator. When the doors opened no one was in there so she jumped in and closed the door. She still had the lobby and the garage to go through. It was well lit, but she was a little apprehensive about that. She made it to her Lincoln Navigator, jumped in, locked the doors and put her seatbelt on. She started up and drove out slowly, she didn't see anyone or anything, so she went on her way. It would be nice to have a nice evening with Ray, they never got to do this very often so, why not.

Gail pulled up and valet parked. As soon as she walked in she saw Ray, as she walked towards him she felt like the whole room was staring at her wondering why was she at their wedding reception. Ray kissed her on the cheek and told her how lovely she looked. I think tonight that I over dressed, what do you think Ray? I think that every man in this room is sad because he, is not me, they have never seen anyone so beautiful, and I am the most luckiest man in the room.

When Ray finally got everything finished and packed up for Adam and Russell to take back to the wharehouse, Ray finally got to come over and sit down and have a drink with Gail. Adam and Russell came in to say that they were leaving and told Gail how beautiful she looked. See you tomorrow boss, Adam said, and then they were gone. "Would you like another drink Gail?" I have to drive home so I probably shouldn't. Well, it just so happens that I have reserved a room for the night, and it's a great room. Small bar, round bed, hot tub, did I already mention a round bed? Gail laughed at him, and they both felt a little pressure of the last couple of weeks being released. What about in the morning, I'll need some scrubs from home and I have 7 o'clock rounds in the morning,

Ms. Boden will have a cow if I'm not there. Well, I took the liberties of going to your place and met your son there and I have brought you two sets to choose from, scrubs, dress, skirt and blouse and your white Doctor's coat. I hope that you don't mind. "What about under clothes, bras, etc...said Gail?" That was the hardest part for me, I didn't want you to wear any, but I brought you two sets to choose from. And what about sleepwear Gail asked? Now those I truly left at home, I think we can get by without those, what do you think? I"m thinking that maybe your right about that, smiled Gail. And what about you Ray, what did you bring? I brought a toothbrush, I only live six blocks from here, I can change in the morning.

After a few more drinks, Gail drank Ginger Ale; and a great steak dinner for the two of them, they retired to bed. Ray asked Gail to wait a minute, that he needed to talk to the chef about something and would be right back. Ray was back in just a couple of minutes and they headed for the elevators. When they reached their room, Ray unlocked the door and gail walked in to see Dozens of roses, candle light everywear, even around the huge deep tub for two, champagne on ice and the bed turned down. "My you sure went to a lot of trouble for us didn't you?" No problem is big or small when it comes to the woman I love. They sat down on the sofa and each had a glass of champagne, when Ray turned to Gail and said, Gail we have been seeing each other for almost two and a half years. During that time, we have seen wonderful day's together, seen sun rises and sunset's. I couldn't love you anymore than I do right now so, I think it's time for me to say, as he dropped down on one knee, will you marry me?" Gail was stunned, she had no idea that this was why he wanted her to come here tonight. It was only fitting since this is where they met.

Gail closed her eyes and tried to think of why she should say no, but when she opened them again, she said "Yes, Yes, I will marry you Raymond Bertolli. Ray reached for his pocket and brought out a little small box (he went to Jared's). It had the most stunning diamond that she had ever seen. It was a wide band and on top was a heart shaped 3 caret diamond and down each side of the band were baquettes of blue and white diamonds, Ray said that they mached her eyes, and they did. She looked Ray right in the eye and said, I truly love you Ray, and I would love to be your wife, and nothing or no one can tear us apart, or take us down. You are the smartest, sweetest, talented, and handsomest man I have ever known, and I promise I will be the best wife and your best friend alway's."Well maybe, Ray stood up and pulled her with him, we could dance a little, while he unzipped her dress, or I can really show you how talented I am as he slipped her from her dress." They finished undressing in the bedroom and was lying on the bed, he kissed her all over her body, every inch and then again. Ray moved on top of Gail and then entered her all at once, it took her breath away. She looked at Ray and said, I love you and you are stuck with me forever now. As to which Ray replied at this point I just want to be stuck in you, and then started to kiss her with such an urgency that Gail matched his one on one. With hot breath's and a lot of sweat later, they had consummated their engagement. Ray got up and went in to shower, Gail followed him in, we do everything together when we can, is it a deal? You bet sweetheart, we both work some crazy hours that we really need to be together, when we can, really make an effort to do this, and we will die old together. When finished in the shower, they went back into the bed and fell into a very deep and much needed rest for both of them.

Chapter 22

Captain Lane woke early and was at his office by 7 a.m. Bob was just getting there too, you couldn't sleep either I take it Bob?" No tossed and turned most of the night, I finally got up so Pat could get some rest. As soon as you see Marshall and Womack come in, tell them that I want to see them. They were right on time and heard him holler out to Bob. "Hey boss, What's up?" Yes please come in and shut the door, Bob, you need to hear this too, so come on in and have a seat. I hear from an informant that a possible hit is going down today, Maybe this afternoon, or maybe tonight, and as you have probably guessed, it's on one of the Bertolli's. We don't know which one, so we need to keep our eyes and our ears opened at all times. The day shift is going to comb the neighborhood, checking rooftops, any empty houses, vacant buildings, or apartments that may be empty. I want the two of you to go home and get some sleep because you are going to need it. I also think that they are setting their sights on anyone of the Bertolli household members. You will need to be extra carefull tonight, I don't want to hear about you two getting shot. You won't Boss, we know how to cover each others back Womack said. I'm not trying to play the big dog here but, Marshall and I practice on this kind of thing all the time. You can bet that we will be careful. Make sure you do said Terry. With that they left to go home to get some sleep.

Marshall could only think of one thing, Joelina Bertolli. He drove towards his house and thought; maybe I'll just stop in the store and get some lunchmeat and snacks for tonight for Womack and himself. Mark pulled into an open parking spot and just sat there, he was as nervous as could be. Finely he got up the nerve to go into the store. He stopped just short of the door when she came out and helped an older gentleman to his car and he just stared, God she was gorgeous. When he finely summed up the courage to go in, there she was at the front counter. "Can I help you sir?" He tried to speak but his mouth froze up. Sir? "Oh yes, I'm sorry, I'd like some lunchmeat for a steak tonight." No, I mean I would like some lunchmeat. "What would you suggest, what makes a good sandwich for hungry men at work?" God, he was blowing it already. "Well, I love the smoked turkey breast;

it's my favorite with bacon, tomato and lettuce, if you like I could make them up for you and put the condiments on the side in packets to put on later. That's great Miss, I need four total, and I'll just go and get some things to go with them. Marshall walked around the store starring at her every chance that he got. He felt someone put his hand on his shoulder from behind, can I help you sir? Oh, no, no I was just waiting for her to make my sandwiches. When he turned around, he saw that it was her uncle Dominic from Sicily."Sir, I'm one of the police officers watching your brother's house in the evening from 7p.m.to 7 a.m. I realize that much,said Dominic, but why are you just standing around starring at my niece?" Well all I can say to that is that she is so beautiful, it's hard not to stare sir. Dominic was starting to grin and that made Mark feel a little bit better. Joelina is my niece and I love her dearly, no one will ever hurt her as long as I'm around said Dominic." Marshall looked at Joelina and then back to Dominic and said, I feel the same way also sir." I would like to talk to her though, whenever my mouth starts working again. Joelina waved him over and bagged his things. Mark could barely count out his change. Dominic was now in full laugh mode. Thank you Miss, you have a nice day. Marshall walked out the door sweating bullets.

"Uncle Dominic, what are you doing laughing at one of our customers?" Sweetheart, he is one of the police officers outside our door everynight. He only came in to check you out. That boy is in love, bad!

Well you know Uncle Dominic, that I am old enough to make my own decisions about men."Really, when was the last time that you were out on a date Joelina?" Have you ever been on a real date at all, asked Dominic?" Well it's only been about humm, eight months ago. The store needs me here, besides, as she walked out of the counter, it's none of your buisness. Joelina got to the door and watched him get into his car. He turned around and waved at her and she just raised her had to him, and then went back into the store."Shut up, just shut up, she was blushing, she didn't think that she ever knew how to blush before until now. Michael came out from behind the back of the store and looked at both of them, what's going on out here? It's nothing Papa, nothing at all, as she looked over at her uncle and just smiled at each other. "Okay, said Michael, just let me know when that young man comes back in so I can meet him too, and with that he returned to the back room." Joelina and her uncle just kept on laughing. They had now formed their bond as uncle and niece.

Chapter 23

Gail and Ray woke up to a wonderful day and the feelings from the night before was unsurpassed, they just stared at each other for a moment and remembered everything from the first time they met until know. They both started grinning at each other then Gail, jumped out of bed and said,"I get the shower first." I have to work and you don't have to until later. Ray caught up to her while she was stepping in the shower, and said, "remember, we spend every minute that we can together, your words, not mine", it will be a hardship for me doing this, day after day, but it is all for love. Oh you, Gail said and then pulled him in the shower with her.

When they finally got dressed and went down to the lobby, Ray told Gail that she had some time for breakfast, so they went in and had a wonderful breakfast together. They were truly in love, Gail had no more doubts about that, as they stared at each other over the table. Ray said to Gail, well dear when do you want to tell your family about us? Your son already knows, I showed him the ring when I picked up your clothes. He is very happy for us, if your sure it's what you want. "Yes, it is." Now, said Gail, what about your family, what will they say? Well, they love you already, I see no problems in the near future and beyond, if I'm happy, their happy. Well Mr. Bertolli, I need to get to the hospital, before I see my patients at the office today. Yes, and for me another day in the freezer for tomorrows ice sculpture. The Cardinals playoff party, and it's here at the Ritz again. Should I keep our room for another night? Gail smiled and said, no, I need to talk to the children about us and also get some house work done. Maybe next time, could I get a rain check on that? Sure you can baby, without a doubt. Why don't you get the Valet to bring our cars around and I'll settle up with our bill, okay? She kissed him goodbye and then went to have their cars brought around. While waiting she walked across the driveway to look at the flowers that were planted in the large pots out front. She was looking at the beautiful arrangement that was in them, when a car speeded up and was headed right for Gail, had it not been for one of the other valets running to push her out of the way, Gail would be dead by now. "Are you alright Gail, said Ray rushing to pick her up?"

Gail got up and dusted off her scrubs and then noticed that the valet was having trouble getting up. "Oh, my, are you alright young man?" He said that the car had clipped him on his right leg, but he thought that he would be fine. Gail asked him if he could walk on it, then they would see. The young man couldn't put his weight on it and Gail called for an ambulance, what's your name sir, Gail asked? My name is Jonny Scott. Is there someone that I can call to meet you at the hospital? "Yes, my mother, if you could." Gail dialed the number that he gave her and let Jonny talk to her so she wouldn't come flying to the hospital. Gail talked with her again and told her that she was a doctor and that he would be fine, and not to rush herself and to stay calm, I know that's hard to do when it's your child, but you don't need to be in an accident too. Jonny's mother thanked Gail, and Gail told her that she would meet her at the hospital.

Ray asked the boy, as he helped him over to one of the chairs out front, if he saw who was driving that car? All Jonny could remember was he had dark hair and a mustache, and the car was a dark grayish blue and that it was a Grande Am or the other car that looks like that. The ambulance pulled up and they took Jonny to the St. Louis University hospital, and Gail told Jonny that she would be down to se him after she saw her patients in the hospital, Gail would add him to her list to see this morning. Ray followed Gail to work, and waited until she was inside before he left. Ray saw a dark colored Grand Am parked on a side street, but before he could get turned around, it was gone.

Chapter 24

When Gail got into the hospital, she went into the doctors lounge and called Captain Lane to let him know what happened. Terry asked her if anyone saw who it was or the make and model of the car. Gail told him that she never saw the car, it came in and out so fast she never got a chance to see it. She gave him Jonny Scott's name and told him that he was here at the hospital, down in emergency and that he could tell him something about it. Terry said that he was on his way over right now, to talk to the boy while it's fresh in his brain. Captain Lane told Gail to stay sharp, keep your eyes wide open because you never know. He was right, she was so happy with her and Ray's engagement that she had let her guard down, that wouldn't happen again! She was feeling a little sick to her stomach though for the past couple of weeks, every since Ray's father came into the hospital and everything going on between her and Ray. Maybe it was the eggs at breakfast, that's all she seemed to want to do is burp eggs. She was sure she would feel better after her rounds this morning.

Gail went in to see Mrs. Youngblood first, and she looked so tired. How are you doing this morning Sherry, Gail asked? Well I never got enough sleep, I was up coughing all night long. Well, that's what you need to do to break that up inside, I know it's an awful thing, but it has to come up, how is the nebulizer going? Does it seem to help at all? Gail walked over and listened to Sherry's back and chest. I'm sorry Sherry, but I can't send you home yet, we still need those medications to work and get some more of that conjestion up and out of your lungs. Yes Dr. McDougal, I know and I'm doing everything that you're telling me to do. I think that we still need you to stay at least one more night here, you still need hooked up to these IV's and they will work faster if you are here, then I will see you in the morning. Thank you Dr. McDougal. Well your very welcome and try and get a little rest, I'm going to add a cough syrup to help with the cough so maybe you might get some sleep. Oh, that would be wonderful, thank you again. No problem, I'll see you tomorrow, and then she was off to see Mr. Hanson.

Good morning sir, and how are you doing today, asked Gail? "Well I don't feel like my heart and my head are running a race if that helps, said Willie! Let's see, we put you on Verapimil 240 for your pulse rate to bring it down, let's check that first, Gail held his wrist and counted, ninety two, wow, what a big difference from one hundred and twenty, two day's ago.I think I'm going to keep you on that for three months and see if that helps you out. Then we changed your Cozaar 100 to Hyzaar 100/50, and also put you on Clonidine 0.1mg every day, let's check your blood pressure, again wow, it was one-forty over ninety five. We still have a way's to go yet, but we'll get you there. Once we get you regulated, things will go a lot faster, do you have any questions for me Willie? No Doctor, I'm just glad that my head isn't throbbing with every heart beat, and for that I thank you. You are welcome Mr. Hanson, if you keep improving, I may let you go home tomorrow, if you promise to take the medications that I have given you. Yes mamm, I sure will. As Gail was writing in Mr. Hanson's chart, she could hear someone having a fit down the hall. Mr. Hanson said that he was glad she wasn't his neighbour, his blood pressure would never go down. One more night and we will see what tomorrow brings Mr. Hanson, we just may get you home. Try and have a restful day and I'll see you in the morning, and with that she was gone.

As Gail walked up to the nurses station to get Ms. Boden's chart, she said good morning ladies, how has she been from last night? About that time she could hear Ms. Boden holloring all the way down the hall. Gail went straight to her room, Ms. Boden, what is going on in here? A young house keeper was in the bathroom almost ready to cry. She wants to help the nurse change my sheet's, with me in the bed, screamed Ms. Boden. "That's because I still have you on complete bed rest until tomorrow? They are just doing their jobs, I'll get you up and put you in the chair." Gail called the nurse's station for someone to come and help her move her to a chair. They were there in seconds, they got her up and into the chair bringing her cath. bag and IV lines with her. The housekeeper changed out the bed and was gone within a minute. I'm going to leave you in this chair for one hour and then I will have the nurses put you back to bed, I think your going to find out why I still had you on bed rest for another day.

I need to speak to about your behavior Ms. Boden, the workers here at this hospital are the legs we stand on, and that position deserves respect, you are rude,obnoxious and hateful to everyone here who is trying to get you well so you can go home. If you continue on this way, I will be forced to dismiss you from my practice and you will need to find another doctor. I will stay on for thirty days until you can find another doctor to get in with. "Do I make myself clear Ms. Boden?" She couldn't say anything, she didn't want to find another doctor, so she agreed that she would work on her additude and anger. All I need said Gail, is just one more complaint and I will dismiss you. She sat up in the chair so Gail could listen to her heart and took her pulse, which was at 115. Gail took he blood pressure and it was 160/98. You need to calm down to get better if you plan on going home and leaving this hospital. Ms. Boden agreed and with that said, Gail left the room. Why do people have to be so hateful Gail thought. Ms. Boden should be a patient of the "Little Natzi" as they called her, it was Dr. Heitzman, barely five foot tall and would be perfect for Ms. Boden, they both had the same additude. Maybe there's more to her problems, maybe she's just lonely.

Chapter 25

Ray went back to his office to get done with the Ice sculpture for the Cardinal party. His best friend Russell, was there already, preparing pastries. "Hey boss, how's it going?" I would have to say pretty darn wonderful, the woman I love, said yes to my proposal. Alright! Man that's great, you do know that you're getting the better end of the deal, don't you? Not only is she a knock out, she's a doctor too. Your a very lucky man Ray. Yes, that's the only thing I do know right now, however she was almost ran over this morning at the Ritz Carlton, while she was waiting for them to bring her car around. "She wasn't hurt was she Ray?" No, but one of the parking valet's was, he pushed Gail out of the way just in time, we had to call an ambulance. Gail's going in to check on him while she's doing her rounds. "Did anyone know who it was?" The valet saw a grayish/blue Grand Am, and that the guy had a black mustache. Russ, you and Adam havn't seen anything different around here have you? Have I what, said Adam as he was walking in? Ray then told the story over to Adam. Both said that nothing seemed out of place that they noticed. "Does this have anything to do with what happened to your father Ray, asked Adam?" I don't know, it could be, maybe that car was meant for me. Well, help me keep an eye out for a while, anything out of the ordinary okay? Sure thing Ray, I mean I'm going to be your best man at your wedding right, I am your best friend and all. We will see when the time comes. Well now I'm really hurt, crushed you have broken my heart, Russ was acting like he was crying, and then they both started laughing. "You know I love my brother, but he's going to have to stand behind you at the church, you have been my best friend since grade school. They both started to tear up now for real. "Okay enough of this serious shit, let's get back to work, times a ticking. Adam, get that Steamboat round into the oven ASAP and you might make the usher list. Let's just all keep each other safe, what do you say guy's? Both said that they would, and then all three got to work for the Cardinal playoff party tonight. Usher my ass, said Adam laughing.

Ray went into his office and called his mother before going back in that freezer to see if it was alright for him and Gail to come over for dinner tomorrow night, Ray didn't mention to her that Joelina had already asked them to come for dinner. "Raymond, you can alway's come here for dinner, everynight if you want to, you should know that by now" After setting up a time, Ray called Gail and left her a message with the time to be there, Gail knew that they were going, he wanted to make sure that she brought extra clothes from home. The Lord has truly blessed Ray again with Gail, after the horrible thing that happened to Vanesa and the baby. He loved Gail very much, but there would alway's still be room for Vanessa and the baby and Gail knew that also, that's what makes Gail even more loving for him.

Ray then made out a final list of to do things and stuck it on the freezer door, as he went into the freezer. Burrr...cold in here, about ten degrees, it's a good thing that he alway's kept a heavy Parka there just for ice sculpting.

Ray's wait staff would be going to the Ritz and start setting up everything for the party, red, white and blue, Cardinals colors. Ray had already talked to his top head waiter and made sure that they knew what they had to do. Ray had a good staff now, people that he could depend on to alway's do the right thing, and of course he pay's them well. He also buy's their uniforms, men and women alike, black dress slacks, white tuxedo shirts, patened black shoes and a black cumberbund with a black bow tie. Ray liked his staff to look and be their finest, it was a reflection on his buisness and Ray himself. Ray liked to be alone in the freezer while doing ice carvings, it gave him time to think, and today it was about Gail, yes he was a lucky man to have a woman like her. He truly did love her, and they were great together.

Chapter 26

Before leaving the hospital, Gail went down and into the Emergency Department to see Jonny and how he was doing. She went up to the desk and asked the nurse which bed that he was in. "He's in room four, bed #2, Dr. McDougal, but he still may be down in x-ray, I'm not sure." Is his mother here, Gail asked? Yes, she is, she's talking to the policeman, did the boy do something wrong, asked Shelby, is that why the police are here? No, he just saved my life, he pushed me out of the way of a speeding car. "Really, no kidding, wow, what a great kid. I'll make sure he gets the royal treatment while he's here. Thank you Shelby, that would be great, he deserves it. Gail then walked down to the room, she walked in and was talking to Jonny's mother she guessed. "Oh Gail right on time, I'd like for you to meet Jonny's mother." Mrs. Scott, this is Dr. McDougal. I'm very pleased to meet you doctor. "No, the pleasures all mine, you and your husband have raisied one heck of a young man."

Jonny saved my life this morning, is he stil in x-ray? Yes, but he should be right back. I wish that I could stay and see him, but I have patients waiting to see me at the office at nine. I have fifteen minutes to get there. Please call me at the office, here is my number, I would really like to know how he is doing. I'll talk to you soon Mrs. Scott, and then Gail left.

Captain Lane Walked out with Gail, did you get a picture of the car, or who was in it? No, replied Gail, I wish I would have so I would know what to watch out for. Jonny only remembers that it was a dark grayish car and the driver had a mustache. Gail, you know that the Bertolli family is haveing some real problems right now, do you think that you could not be around them as much, at least not until this grudge match is over? "Gail said,I don't think that's possible, you see Ray and I got engaged last night." We do however vow to be more alert and careful from now on. Well, I hope you know what your doing. Yes, for the first time in a long time, something feels right, she just hoped that everything would work out sooner and not later. Captain Lane told Gail to call him if anything, no matter if it seems silly, or not. Gail told him that she would and then she left the building.

When Gail got to her car, she noticed a man looking around the parking lot, she went back in and told Terry about it. They walked out together and Gail pointed him out. Well Gail, I don't think he will hurt you, that's my friend Bob, he is also a police officer, he's with me checking out any cars around to see if they match the description of the car from this morning. Well I still feel better knowing that he is out there. Thank you so much Terry, and then she got in her car and headed for her office.

Chapter 27

While Joelina ran errands, that left Michael and Dominic in the store. Christina had just left to go and fix dinner for Maria's family. Dominic, said Michael, I hope you like Baked chicked, mashed potatoes, green beans, dinner rolls and peach pie for dessert? How do you know what we are having for dinner, asked Dominic? I saw the grocery list that Joelina had, men tend to know after so many years of marriage, and then if you don't like it, you can eat it or starve, and do I look like I have missed any meals, said Michael? Dominic laughed and said as a matter of fact, he said rubbing his belly, we could both stand to lose a little weight, then they both started laughing.

They were still laughing when Joelina came back from her errands and deliveries. "What's so funny Papa? Uncle Dominic, did you say something about the policeman to Papa? No Joelina, we were talking about your mother's cooking and how we could both stand to lose some weight."Why do you think we were talking about your boyfriend Joelina? Have we missed something? Have you been kissing and not telling? HUMM! "Oh, Uncle Dominic, you are out of control, Joelina stomped her foot then went to stock some shelves. "Dominic, you must watch that stomp, she gets that from our Mama, remember?" I do now, they both grinned at Joelina and kept smiling for a while, remembering things of the past.

Why do men alway's have to be so irritating, Joelina asked herself. I have no boyfriend, he is a police officer and is probably married anyway, but she had to admit that he is a very handsome man. She shook her head, she had no time for such things, Papa and Mama needed her in the store and someday, she will take it over from them. Joelina remembered when she was in grade school, alway's coming in after school, wanting to work the cash register, but was usualy sent to the back to help stock shelves with Maria and Angelina, yes fond memories. Could she really marry a police officer? No way, I'm thinking about him again she thought. Why can't I stop thinking about him? Papa and Uncle Domonic just distracted her for a while, but she had to admit that she liked what she saw of that man. Okay, no more policeman; she had to be ready for dinner tonight with Maria's family and tomorrow night with Raymond and Gail, then the following night with Angelina's family. That was one of the errands, getting everyone set up for dinner and conversation, hopefully so she and her "cohort" Uncles, might pick up on something that they would say and not know if it could help or not, just get them to talking and see what comes out. That was Joelina's part, getting them all over so the Uncles could casually start the conversation. She let her Mama know about Ray and Gail for tomorrow's dinner and Angelina's family the following night. Yes, said Christina, while she was still at the store. I spoke with Raymond today and he told me that they were coming for dinner tomorrow night. Joelina thought to herself, maybe she could invite the policeman to dinner some night. No, what was wrong with her, she had to stop thinking about him, she needed to stay focused for now, no distractions, none! Her family was in trouble and she needed to help as much as she could.

Chapter 28

Captain Lane left the hospital and went back to the station with Bob. While in the car Bob said, are you ever going to tell me what's going on, or am I suppose to stand out in the parking lot to be run over? "Well, what is it Terry?" Bob this is under wraps, okay, you talk about this to no one but me is that understood? Sure, you know me Terry, we have known each other when we came on the force together. Alright, this comes from one of my best informents from the soup kitchen down on tenth street. One of the Bertolli's may be killed tonight, but I don't know which one, all he had was the last name. he also said that the man was with another man and the one who did the most talking had a mustache. Dr. McDougal was almost run over this morning after becoming engaged to Raymond Bertolli last night. They were at the Ritz Carlton. One of the valet parkers got hit pushing Gail out of the way just in time."Is that why you had me in the parking lot at the hospital, to find that Grand Am you told me about?" Yes, that was the reason. "I'm sorry now that I didn't see that car. That car could have been meant for Ray, we don't know for sure.

Ray Bertolli, is a very smart man, he not only own his buisness alone, he also has his Batchlors and Masters Degree in buisness, he takes care of his own books, and saves a lot of money, you should of seen that ring, I thought it was going to put my eye out it had so many diamonds. I hope my wife doesn't ever see it or I will get that look that say's, I need a new diamond. I'll never be able to afford to buy one like Dr. McDougal's. Maybe we should start our own catering buisness, what do you think Boss, said Bob? Mr. Bertolli has worked very hard to get where he is at today, or I should say tonight. "What do you mean tonight Terry?' He is catering the playoff party for the St Louis Cardinals tonight at the Ritz Carlton in Clayton. Maybe we should go down there tonight and interview Mr. Bertolli, get some autographs, what do you think Terry? I'm already two steps in front of you Bob, we have four seats ready for us, compliments of Mr. Ray Bertolli and I had Gail call him so he wil know that we will be there watching out for him, you never know how this crazy bastard is. You said four seats, who else is going with us? Our wifes will be coming with us, I had Debbie call your wife and let her know, you do have a tuxedo don't you Bob? They were pulling into the station house now. Yes, as a matter of fact I do, I hope it still fits, well, maybe I could rent one. I think I'll call my wife. Terry just started laughing at that one. We get the fun one, but we still have to be on our toes. Bob went to call his wife Pat, it was only two o'clock, maybe she could get someone to run his things down to him here at the station. Hello, Pat, Babe do you think that my tuxedo is okay for me to wear tonight? I think it will be fine, our son Rick is on his way there now with everything you will need, said Pat. Thank you sweetheart, thank God for his wife of 35 years, she knows how to take care of her man, I'll see you soon.

Marshall and Womack will be watching the Michael Bertolli home and we will have cruisers covering the childrens houses. "You're alright Terry, I don't care what they say about you." I don't care either, if they're talking about me they are leaving someone else alone. Terry headed for his office and told Bob to have Marshall and Womack come in to see him before they went back out again and also change by six o'clock to go to the Ritz. Should I go and pick up my wife? Yes, unless you plan on walking! "No Bob, I called for a limo to pick up our wives, and then us last." You know Terry, it's nice to know that my wife takes orders from you too. They both got a big laugh out of that one.

Marshall and Womack were just coming in at six, to be breifed before they went back out to the Bertolli home. They stopped at their lockers and then went up to see the Captain. Hello men, said terry, how's it going? You tell us, you and Bob are walking around like penguins, where are you two going to the Ritz? Well, smart-ass as a matter of fact, we are. Cardinal's Playoff Party. "Man why wern't we invited, we love the team. We, said Terrry, will be on official duty tonight on Mr. Raymond Bertolli. His fiance', Dr Gail McDougal was almost ran over today, maybe meant for Ray, we don't know. Here's the layout, the day officers got ready for you, the only place that anyone could really hide in is just two doors down from the Bertolli house Watch the windows and ask the family to try and stay away from them also, do you need anything else? Well, we could use some autographs from the team, Pujols, Larussa, even Fred bird, we'll take anything. Terry and Bob were laughing as they walked out, leaving Womack and Marshall wishing it was them going to the Ritz. "Man, Marshall said, how did they get invited?" Womack said, maybe when we haveover twenty-five years on the forse, we'll get the invites for all the great things, or not.

Chapter 29

Gail got home early from work for the first time in days. She opened up all the windows to get some fresh air circulating through the house. Her plants were in bad shape; I do not do well with houseplants, or any plants for that matter, Gail thought. Gail had once killed a cactus and a mother-in-laws tounge, how's that for gardening? She went about vacuuming, dusting and doing the laundry and it got her to thinking, I'd have one more to take care of besides herself, now that her and Ray were getting married. Gail loved the thought of marring Ray, she truly loved him, she knew that for sure. She will be proud to be his wife, after all when it is said and done Ray kept a cleaner house than she did, that was a good thing. Gail had just started the washing machine when the phone rang.

Hello? Mom, it's me how are you doing, said Katie? I'm just great now, I'm so happy that you called, I have some news for you, I wish you were here when I tell you this. "What is it

Mom, don't let me get freaked out, you know how things stress me out." Well, my darling daughter, your mother has just become engaged to Mr. Ray Bertolli as of last night. "Mom, are you kidding?" That is so awesome, I am happy for you. Ray is such a great guy and he's getting the best woman in the world. Oh' Katie, I wish you were here with me right now. Well your wish is coming true, I'll be home Tuesday night for about two weeks. "Katie, thats wonderful." Mom, don't go all out while I'm there, I'll be working at the America Center downtown for the fashion show, next Thursday threw Sunday, so don't make a lot of plans. "Well can I at least plan on you having dinner out with Ray and I one night before you go back to Chicago?" Yes mother you can, just not on those days that I mentioned. I want to see Steven while I'm home also, maybe the four of us can catch dinner and a movie one night, what do you think Mom? That would be fine. I'm free for six days after the fashion show, we can catch up on some things, maybe have a carpet picnic, just us girls, you can ask Aunt Lynn and I"ll invite Diane. "What are you doing now Mom?" Well I haven't been home for two day's; so I'm cleaning house, and now I'll add your room to the list, you know just change the sheets and dust. Well don't go all out for me Mom, you alway's have a clean house and don't know it.

Well I have to go Mom, I'm meeting Diane for dinner tonight, she drove up today and will go back tomorrow, I miss seeing her everyday, we've only been best friends since second grade. "Okay sweetie, you still have your key just in case I'm not here when you get home don't you?" Yes, I do, hey, how about ordering Pizza Tuesday when I get in so you and I will have more time to catch up on things. Sounds wonderful Katie, and wait until you see my ring. Ray picked it out all by himself and done a perfect job of it. Well I have to go Mom, Dianes waiting, I'll see you Tuesday around six o'clock, I love you Mom. I love you too Katie, see you then. I can't wait to see you and that ring too, bye Mom.

As Gail hung up the phone, she reflected back on her childhood friend, and it was her own sister Lynn. They were the closest growing up together, barely a year between them. Gail remembered the time that Lynn fell out of a swing and broke her arm. Gail went screaming for their mother. They took her to the hospital and she has to this day a long scar down her arm where they had to put a metal brace in her arm to hold it together. They also got to paint their room how they wanted it when they got older. They painted it black and white, they dipped their hands in the paint (just their palms) and put them on the walls and made a footprint out of a sponge and used our fingers for the toes, we put them on the floor and the ceiling, then we had a blck light, we thought that we were so cool, we loved it. Gail knew how Katie felt about Diane, that's how Gail felt about Lynn. Gail was so excited about Katie coming home that she started up the stairs to do her room right now. She got halfway up the stairs when the phone rang again, it was Ray. "Hi baby, hows the most beautiful girl in the world?" I'm just fine, I just got off of the phone with Katie, and she's coming home next Tuesday for two weeks. She has a fashion show at the America Center downtown Thusday threw Sunday the first week and the next week she is all open. She wants to get together with you me and Steven, and catch dinner and a movie one night, whens good for you babe? I can do Wednesday,or the following Monday or Thursday said Ray. Now all I need to do is talk to Steven and set a date and time. Let me know after you talk to your son sweetheart and we can set a date before I would book another party or something. I will, hows your parents getting along with your Uncles? "Well every since my mother put her foot down to my uncles, things have been going well. Uncle Vincent and Uncle Dominic take turns going to the store with Papa each day. "Do they still think that there is a threat to your family?" Yes, I'm afraid so. When we go out to dinner lets go on your side of the Mississippi, so as not to get your family involved anymore than it is now.

Have you found out anymore about Jonny, Ray asked? Yes, I went down to see him before I came home. He has a torn ligament in his left knee and some bruising, but he will be fine. He will need to do some therapy and be off of work, but his Employer (The Ritz) is going to still pay him while he is off, they said that Jonny was a true hero and that he went above and beyond the call of duty to take care of his customers, It probably didn't hurt any, that you do a lot of your parties there either Gail laughed. When he's up to it why don't we take him out to dinner with his parents some night, how does that sound Gail? We have time before he will want to get better and be able to walk into someplace and not have to use crutches, but I'll keep an eye on him and talk to his parents also. Sounds great, just keep me informed.

Well dear, I'm going to take a shower, watch a little football, then I'm going to bed. I wish you were here with me. Gail replied that it wouldn't be that much longer, you can count on that. You have a great night and I'll see you over at Mom and Pop's for dinner tomorow night. Oh, that's right, I'm glad you reminded me, about six-thirty right? Yes dear it is, I love you and I'll see you tomorrow. I love you too Ray, goodnight.

Gail was feeling all tinkly inside Ray, the engagement, Katie coming home, and dinner out with Ray, Katie and Steven, wonderful. What a great day this has been. She finished with the rest of her chores, closed all the windows and locked up and set the alarm. She was on her way up to the shower and do some reading before bed. Gail had no idea the way her life was about to change.

Chapter 30

Michael and Dominic came home from the store and Dominic said, I smell peach pie and baked chicken, we'll see if you are right Michael. Christina came out of the kitchen and said, yes you do, also smashed potatoes, gravy, vegetables and dinner rolls, and I hope you are hungry. She went back into the kitchen and Joelina came out to set the table for everyone, about then the door bell rang. Since when does Maria ever ring the door bell said Joelina, I'll get it.

WhenJoelina opened the door and saw officer Marshall, her jaw dropped to her chest she felt, she stood there, then finally was able to talk."Please come in sir, how can we help you?" Marshall stepped into the parlor and shook hands with all three Bertolli brothers, and introduced himself to them all. "Please sit down officer Marshall, can you stay for dinner, asked Michael?" No thank you sir, I'm on duty now and that's what has brought me in to see you this evening. My captain asked me to tell you all to please stay away from the windows if possible and as much as you can, don't make yourself a target. Alway's keep your eyes open and don't open the door before looking out to see who it is. He was looking at Joelina when he said that. "Maria and her family are coming for dinner, I thought it was them Joelina stated." Well, no harm done, I'll leave you to your dinner. Maybe another night for dinner young man, asked Dominic? Maybe sir, yes I'd like that very much, and with that said ,he was gone. What a nice young man Michael said, it's nice and comforting to know that he is outside helping a family he doesn't really know isn't it Joelina? Well I thought he was rude, implying that I never look before opening the door. "Well sweetheart, did you know it was him, because the look on your face said that you didn't, Michael said." Oh! You men are alway's sticking up for each other, when are you going to learn that I can take care of myself! She looked out the window, hummp, she could take care of herself no matter what these men, or the ones in the car thought about it. The doorbell rang and she went to answer it, she did however look out first before opening the door to her sister's family. Michael and Dominic looked at each other and just smiled. Dominic told Vincent that he would tell him later.

Maria, how are you, said Christina, and how are you too Erik? Just find Mama, and hungry. Well, you will not go away from this house hungry tonight Christina said. They all gathered around the large table that Joelina had set up for and Michael said the blessing tonight before the meal. While the Bertolli's were eating dinner, someone was watching from the second story window of a vacant apartment building. Let just one of them stick their head out the door or come to a window, that's all he needed was one shot. Marshall got back into the car and took up his position again, the same as Womack but facing the other way. You know Mark, we should invest in these old houses around here, all they really need is some TLC and they would be ready to move into. "Hey Marshall, why did you tell me not to bring any lunch tonight?" I probably would of had peanut butter and jelly, but that's alright. Someone fix us dinner tonight? Please don't tell me that you cooked. No, I bought these today at the Bertolli's store on Market street, as he passed Dave's sandwiches back to him. It's a turkey BLT on wheat buns. Look at these baby's they're huge. Who fixed them for you? NO, don't tell me, the young hot chick from the top story over there, as he nodded towards the Bertolli house. "Yeah, so do you want it or not, because I"ll eat them, if you don't want any." No way dude are you getting this back, do you have any mayo by chance? Mark threw him a couple packets along with chips, soda and hostess cup cakes. Dave didn't say another word, he was too busy eating and enjoying each bite. Dave kept watch on the empty building with some of the windows broken out, he spanned the area, and saw nothing. So Mark, have you asked her out yet? I'm working on it; her father and uncles want me to come to dinner some night when I'm off duty. What about me, they didn't invite me? Now I'm crushed, Dave said laughing. You were not at the door tonight when I asked them to stay out of the windows. Captains ordders, not mine, someone had to tell them.

Chapter 31

Ray came out of the freezer about every ten to fifteen minutes or so, but he would still be chilled to the bone. He would drink hot tea or coffee, whatever was ready to help warm him up, he would also hang his parka up over the stoves to keep it warm for the next time he had to go in the freezer again. Ray only had a couple more times in there and he will be done for the party tonight. The ice carving was a large baseball, with a Cardinal bird sitting on top with a baseball bat, just like they have on their shirts. Ray needed to be at the Ritz tonight by seven at the very latest, everyone else had already left the building. When Ray was just about ready to go back in for the last time, he remembered some paperwork that he needed for the owner's of the Cardinal's. He was also thinking about Gail, and the look on her face when he proposed to her, priceless! Gail is the woman for me thought Ray. Tomorrow his parents would know, and he already knew what they will say, "It's about time."

Ray's family already loved Gail. Ray looked at the clock in his office, he needed to get going, he only had a couple more things he needed when, BAMM...what was that? Ray went back into the kitchen when he heard the freezer door shut. Adam, did you forget something? Russell? Ray went over to the freezer and opened the door, what are you...at that moment someone pushed him into the freezer and shut the door. All right you guy's this really isn't funny, Ray said as he tried to open the freezer door, I don't have my parka on in here. Someones just about to lose their job if this door doesn't open in five seconds. It's not funny anymore, just open the door. No answer. Ray tried his cell phone but, couldn't get a signal in there. they say dial 911 and they will be able to find you and search you out, he hoped so. He dialed 911 and then sat his phone on top of a box of sirloins. He had some empty potato sacks that he used for his ice carvings so he wrapped himself up in those, he sat on another big box to get his feet off of the steel floor. He looked at his watch, five- forty five

they should all be at the Ritz now getting set up. Now he was getting nervous, two minutes and the hair in his nose were frozen, also his eyebrows. Who is playing this kind of trick...? His words trailed off, Papa, could it be the same person who tried to kill Papa? Someone should come soon he hoped, but everyone on his staff should be there setting up. Ray prayed for a miracle.

Russell and Adam were sitting everything up when Adam noticed that they has forgotten the Canned Heat on the loading dock, at the wharehouse. Russ, keep it going, I have to run back to the wharehouse and get the Canned Heat we forgot on the loading dock. I'll keep them working said Russell. Adam went out the door, just as Cindy, one of their waitresses was walking in carrying the box of Canned Heat. "Where did you get these Cindy?" I was on my way back to get them. Cindy said, some guy in a gray car said that you forgot these. Yes, I did but who was the man that dropped them off? I don't know he had a black mustache and was driving that grayish blue looking car, I have never seen him before. Adam tried to call Ray's cell number, but got no answer so he tried the shops phone, same thing. Cindy, please take these into Russell and tell him what you told me, and then Adam ran to his van.

Ray was trying to stay calm, but it was hard to think of anything else but getting out of here. He sat up some boxes and wrapped them around him too. I hope someone misses me soon, Ray thought. Now he knew how the homeless people must feel, if he ever makes it out of here alive, he will do more for them that's for sure.Maybe open a soup kicthen, and serve from eleven to three in the afternoon. His staff could use the extra money and the homeless would get warm and have a free meal. He would talk to Russ about it, that's if he ever get's out of here.

Chapter 32

Dinner at the Bertolli house was going fine with Maria and her family. Watching Michael with his family, Dominic wished that he would have settled down but, at the same time he didn't want anything to happen to another woman like what happened to Vanessa, he would alway's be watching over his shoulder like he was with Michael's family now. Still he wanted that dream. Joelina was day dreaming and didn't hear her Uncle Vincent ask for the potatoes twice. Joelina!, said Maria, pass the potatoes to Uncle Vincent! Oh, I'm sorry, my mind must be on something else. "Are you sure it's not on "someone" else?" asked Michael. Joelina looked at her Uncle Dominic and said, what are you starring at? "Only a young lady who looks like she's in love." "In love!" "Are you crazy?" I have no time for such foolery; now talk about something else please. Vincent was looking at Joelina and he saw it too, the look in her eyes, he looked over at Dominic and nodded to across the street and Dominic shook his head yes, so she was thinking about the nice police officer who had come to the door earlier. That would be something new, a police officer in the Bertolli family, maybe it's time for a change.

To change the subject, Vincent asked Maria what she had been doing to keep herself busy. "You mean besides watching these hellions all day?" Everyone laughed. I do volunteer work at the parish for the homeless. We make sure that they have at least one good meal a day, I wish we could do more. "And Erik, how is your job coming along?" My job is pretty secure these days, taking peoples money, so they can make more. I hear, said Uncle Dominic, from a little birdie that you are the new department head now at Smith and Barney here in town. Yes, but only temporary for thirty day's to see if it's what I want to do or not. "Now, I wonder who you could of heard that from, as he was looking at Maria and smiling." I'm sorry sweetheart, but I'm just so proud of you. And proud you should be, said Christina, now everyone eat before it gets cold.

After dinner, Dominic said that he would give the girls a break and went into the kitchen with Christina, he knew better than to tell Christina to go and put her feet up, she would tell him that this is her house and she knows how to do dishes. That was very nice of you Dominic, and I will take all the help I can get, thank you she said with a smile.

Little Michael was watching the Animal Planet about black bears, he loved to watch anything that had animals in it. Who knows, maybe he would work at the Zoo with his Uncle Roberto. Daniel is a couch potato, and if he wasn't asleep on his grandfathers lap, he would be fighting Michael over the remote.

While Maria and Joelina played with the children, Joelina rememberd that she still had some Barbie dolls and clothes that Melissa could play with. Joelina went up the stairs to get them. Uncle Vincent went outside to smoke his cigar and Michael was asleep in the chair with little Daniel on his lap, asleep also.

Vincent walked around the house and through the back gate, he never was one to sit still for very long, and he needed to strech his legs.As he walked back around the house to the front, he noticed the policeman watching him and the house. About that time, they both jumped up and hollered for him to get down or inside fast. Vincent barely got in the front door when a bullet rang out and then you heard glass break from an upstairs window. Vincent cried; Oh no, please not Joelina!

Chapter 33

Gail had a long day of cleaning house and doing laundry. She was very happy to have her daughter coming home for two weeks, Gail thought that she will have Pat cancell patient's for a couple of days, but to get them in asap, even if they had to overbook them. Gail knew that Dr. Mucci would cover her hospital rounds for her, she just needed someone to cover for patients that are ill. She could try to reschedule the rest. Maybe Dr. Kane would, she would give him a call in the morning or at the hospital.

Gail needed to call Steven, he answerd on the third ring. Hello; how are you son? I'm just fine Mom, how are you? Wonderful, guess who's coming home for two whole weeks? Let's see, maybe Katie?"Yes! Katie." I'm calling to try and set a date for all of us to go out to dinner, Ray's good for next Wednesday or the following Monday or Thursday, any of those day's good for you son? Well probably Wednesday would be good for me, due to my shift change right now Mom. Okay, I'll pencil us in on Wednesday night at seven, I'll give Ray a call and make sure. Now, where would we like to go, got any ideas? Well you know that Katie will want to go to Red Lobster, but don't let her get away with that. I'm thinking more along the lines of Tony's downtown Alton, their pepper loin is the bomb. You know, Ray loves those too. I personally love the lemon buttered codfish, so, Tony's it is. Katie can surely find something on the menu to eat. Say is there anything you want to tell me Ma? Something about a ring maybe? Oh, Steven I almost forgot. I said yes, you do like Ray don't you? Yes, Ray's a great guy, but I can't say I like going through your underware drawer, next time he's going in on his own. Steven, you are so funny,but really thank you for helping things along. No problem Mom, but I have to go. Works calling me, gotta go catch the bad guys, love you Ma. I love you son, and please be careful, bye.

Gail tried to call Ray but couldn't get through, He was probably at the Ritz tonight already, she would talk to him in the morning. Gail looked at the clock, it was already seven-forty-five. My she had a long day. She would go up and take a shower and relax, maybe get a chance to read that new book she's been trying to read for a month. It was a murder mystery, something out of her normal range, but it looked good in the bookstore, she would give it a try.

Gail was locking up for the night, when her sister Darlene pulled into the driveway. "Hello sis, your out a little past your bedtime aren't you? I just need to vent, I tried to call but the phone was busy. Well there went that book. Come on in, would you like a drink? No, I better not; I'd want to go club my husband over the head or something else crazy like that. "Okay, no drinks for you, tea it is. I'll go put the kettle on said Gail. Once Gail got her sister calmed downand they both had some tea, she asked Darlene what was going on? He is just alway's on my nerves, day and night. "He's the one who should be drinking tea Gail." He has been drinking about a case of beer a day, that's twenty four cans a day. Then he wants to argue about anything and everything I do or say. "I'm never right about anything, he say's. Gail just listened to her sister talk; maybe she would have it out of her system before going home. While she was listening and thinking Gail thought about all the times that she had to vent before. That's what sisters are for, Lord knows I've been there.

After a while, and a few cups of tea later, Darlene was so much better. Well Gail, you've heard all of my problems tonight, what's your's? Gail couldn't wait to tell Darlene. "Ray asked me to marry him and I said yes!" You alway's said that you would never marry again said Darlene, what happened to change all of that? Plain and simple, I love him, and look at the ring that he picked out all by himself, and I just knew. "Oh, my goodness look at all those diamonds, I can't beleive I never noticed them by now, their almost blinding." Please be happy for me Darlene, I truly do love this man. He's everything I want and need in my life. "Do the kids know yet?" Yes, and they both approve, we're taking them out to dinner next Wednesday to Tony's. Wow, Tony's, he must be good.

Darlene and Gail started talking about their childhood and how they both missed their parents. You just never know how things come about after losing your parents, it's never the same. Darlene said that when she see's children smart mouthing their parents, she wants to just kick them in the ass, because when your parents are gone, that's it, you don't get a new set. We were so happy to know love with our family, Darlene said, sometimes it's the parents fault for letting them get by with everything. Gail thought about the Bertolli family and what was happening with them right now. She prays everynight that things will turn around for them soon, back to normal. Darlene got up and said her godbyes for the night, and Gail promised her that she would have her over to lunch one afternoon while Katie was home. Walking Darlene to the door, "Gail told her to just go home and go to bed, then she wouldn't have to listen to him anymore tonight." They both started laughing, Goodbye sis, I love you, Gail told her. I love you too, thanks for letting me vent. Any time you know you are welcome here, goodnight. Gail closed the door and finished locking up and setting the alarm, then up the stairs to bed, she was really feeling tired alot more these days, maybe from all the stress going on right now.

Chapter 34

Ray was afraid that he was going to die tonight in that freezer. Surely someone would miss him and start asking questions. He lay down on some boxes of meat and was trying hard not to fall asleep. He kept thinking about Gail and how she was going to be a widow even before she was a bride. Ray also thought about Vanessa and the baby, maybe he'll see them before the night is over.

All at once the door flew open and Adam grabbed Ray and pulled him out of the freezer, Ray couldn't walk by himself. "Why did you lock me in the freezer, Ray asked Adam?" Ray could hardley speak. He just kept starring at Adam. "I didn't Ray, but someone came in here after we had all left, and put the sharping steel in the door so you couldn't get out. "I'm so cold my ears and my feet hurt." They're probably a little frost bit, I need to take you to the hospital Ray. "Oh no you won't, I have a party to do and I'm not going to miss it." "Do you think you could pull that ice

sculpture out here for me?" I don't think I want
to go in there as of yet.Ray pulled on his Parka,
pulled the hood over his head and put his hands
in the pockets, and was warm so fast it was
unbelieveable how good it felt, he was glad that
he kept it over the ovens.

Ray's hands could hardly hold on to his
tools to finish it for tonight, but he got it done,
probably due to he kept his hands under his
armpits to stay warm, and getting his feet off of
the steel floor probably helped his feet. Adam
called Russell and told him that they were on
their way, Ray didn't want them to worry, this
party had to go well. Russell said that everything
was going fine, no problems, they were set up
and ready to go. Ray just loved his crew, they
knew thier jobs well. "Adam, how long was I in
the freezer, it felt like hours? Only about fifteen to
twenty minutes at the most, I'm guessing but, no
more than that because we were here not long
ago ourselves. Adam started telling Ray about
them all leaving and then that he had forgot the
Canned Heat on the loading dock. When he was
coming back to get it, that's when Cindy came
in carrying it. I asked her where she got it and
she said that some guy with a black mustache
and black hair stopped out front and asked her
to take it in, He was driving a grey car Cindy told
him. Does that sound familiar Ray? "Yes it does,

said Ray taking in some hot coffee to help warm him up, his ear tips and his finger tips still were tingling. I jumped back into the van and got here as soon as I could, said Adam. I'm grateful to you Adam, and thank you for staying on the ball, I owe you my life for your quick thinking. Okay, new rule, everyone leaves together, now let's get this party started, if you could help me with the carving, we can be on our way. There are a couple of guests there that I need to talk to.

Chapter 35

Womack and Marshall were in their usual places, made comfortable with a few pillows from home, and checking out the area. "Hey Marshall, did you get to see your woman when you went to the door tonight?" As a matter of fact I saw (not my woman) but a young lady named Joelina. "Did you drool all over yourself, or could you acually speak?" You know I'm getting a little tired of your shit Womack, so just shut up. Now you know that's not going to happen any time soon, don't you, Dave said.

Marshall rose up just enough to see Vincent Bertolli go around the back of the house. What in the hell was he doing out taking a stroll, knowing the danger he could be in. Womack jumped up too, but not because of Vincent Bertolli. Marshall, lock and load'em buddy, we got a rifle in the upstairs broken window to my left. Marshall tried to sneek out the car door without being seen, but Womack could tell that the way the rifle was pointing, that he didn't get by with it. Womack

149

jumped out and started running to the vacant building where the rifleman was. Marshall hollered for Vincent to get down, or in the front door. Now! That's when he heard the rifle shot. Mark looked at Dave, but he was already in the building where the rifleman was. Two shots rang out from the building, those were from a pistol, Mark followed as back up, he also radioed for back up to Tenth and Market street. Shots fired, shots fired, send an ambulance and backup. Mark hoped that they wouldn't need the bus, but he wasn't taking any chances on his partners life. By the time Mark started in the building, Dave was walking down the stairs with a man in hand cuffs. "I wasn't doing anything officer, I was just trying to stay warm." Yeah right, and I'm the Easter Bunny, move it or lose it mister. Is there another person in the building Dave? There was but he slipped out a side door, I got two shots fired off and I know that I hit him at least once, there's blood on the sidewalk. I heard tires squeal before you hit the bottom step, but, I have the rifle and this Italian jerk. Mark looked over at Dave and said, you got this Dave? Yeah, sure here comes our backup already , go and check on everyone inside. Mark ran out of the vacant building and into the Bertolli house without even knocking, he saw where that shot hit in the upstairs window, please Lord, let her be alright.

When Mark got inside he didn't see Joelina, where is she, he asked? Dominic pointed upstairs with Vincent. Marshall took the stairs two at a time, calling out her name. When he got to the door, there she stood shaking in her uncles arms, her brother-in-law was there also. Joelina looked over to Mark and he took her out of Vincents arms and held her while she cried, Vincent and Erik went down and let them have some time alone. Joelina said that now she knew why he told them to stay away from the windows, and that she was sorry if she was rude to him earlier. Mark held her for a while and kissed her on her forehead. Joelina pulled back away from him and said, don't you think that it's time I know your first Name? It's Mark, my name is Mark Marshall, and then he held her close to him.

Mark could see why the shooter missed his target, the lamp was on the floor and it changed the pattern on the wall by a foot or more."Do you alway's have this lamp on the floor?" Joelina told Mark that she needed to see in the closet, so I set it down on the floor to get some dolls out for Melissa to play with, I was just coming out of the closet when the shot came through her window. I'm so glad that Melissa wasn't up here with me she loves to stand and look out that window. Mark walked Joelina down the stairs and into her mothers arms, they all surrounded her. Mark walked outside to check on Dave, he was fine, thank God. Everyone was okay except for one of the shooters, and he was cuffed and in a squad car. "Well, we got one and one got away, theres a blood trail that goes around the corner and then it stops, that's the car that squealed it's tires that got away. Is everyone in the house alright Dave asked? Yes, they are fine, just pretty shakin' up, Joelina was up there when the window was shot through, thank God she was in the closet looking for some toy's for her neice when it happened. Mark said, Dave we need to go and talk with the Bertolli"s now about the one here in the car and the one that got away. "Johnson, could you take this one down and book him for me, attempted homicide, I'll be down when my shift is over?" Sure thing Womack, take all the time you need.

Mark and Dave walked back into the Bertilli house to talk with Michael and his brothers. Mr. Bertolli said Mark, we have one person in custody and one got away. Dave said, I was able to get off two rounds and I know that I hit him once with my revolver so we don't know how badly he is hurt, he made it to a car that they had parked around the corner. We have the police station checking for any gunshot wounds, just in case he would go and seek help for it. I'll need all three of you brothers to come down to the station in the morning around ten, to see if you may know this man, we will have him in a line up to see if you have ever seen him before. It's a good thing that the unknown suspect was already gone, Dominic wanted to kill that man now. You wil get a chance to see him through a two way mirror. Yes, whatever you need for us to do Mark, may we call you Mark? Mark told them that it would be fine. Officer Marshall seems so formal now don't you think? And Officer Womack, what do you want us to call you. Dave would be just fine sir. Thank you so much for taking your lives in danger for us and everyone else, said Michael, God bless you both! I am so happy that you have saved my family, again thank you.

When Mark walked out of the kitchen, he walked over to Joelina, she was shaken but, was doing fine now. Maria and Eric took their family and went home.Joelina told Mark that she told the children that the window just fell out and scarred me, they don't need to know anything more than that. Dave walked over and told Mark that he would be back in thr car, only parked across the street and farther down. What does he mean, are you still going to watch my house, and why? Why is because there were two people and one got away.Joelina started to shake again and Mark held her and whispered to her sweetly, your Uncles are going to be on watch until we get this thing figured out and taken care of, you'll be safe with them here, he looked over to Vincent and he nodded back to Mark. You will be safe, I promise you, I'll come back and check on you when I can okay? Thank you so much Mark, she blushed and said, it seems so funny not calling you Officer Marshall anymore. I'll see you as soon as I can as he walked out the door. Good night Mark! ..

Mark walked over to the police car and asked if the creep that they took to the station was saying anything yet. He's not saying anything except he want's his Lawyer. "Good because he is going to need one." Dave told Mark that he called Cunningham and Chappel to take watch the rest of the night. We need to get down to the station and start calling hospitals, and clinics to check for any gunshot wounds. I also need to call Captain Lane, he didn't want to call him and ruin his night just yet, besides, they might get an autograph or two.

Mark went back into the Bertolli house and told Joelina to try and get some rest tonight, he would see her sometime tomorrow, not sure when because he would be up all night trying to track the other guy down. How about noon or one o'clock, would that be Okay? Yes, said Joelina, that would be fine, she was going to stay home all day with her Uncle Dominic, while her Uncle Vincent went to the store with Her mother and father. Christina walked up to Mark and said, God has blessed us with you,Mark, as with the Mark in the Bible, you are a saint to me and I will pray for you everyday, now and forever. Thank you, Mrs. Bertolli, now I must sat goodnight to you both, and with that he was out the door.

Chapter 36

Ray and Adam had just got to the Ritz Carlton when the party was just coming in for appetizers and drinks. Ray, with the help of Adam, got the ice sculpture set up and then ray sprinkled red glitter all over the bird on top of the baseball, he learned of this from another Chef, the glitter acually stay's in it's place as the ice melts. Ray went into the kitchen for last minute checks. Everything was ready, so he called his whole staff into the kitchen for a fast meeting. He told them all what had happened and he thanked Cindy with a kiss on her cheek for being good at details of the man in the car. Then he thanked Adam for coming to the rescue and saved his life. Those few minutes saved me from certain death. We now have a new rule, everyone leaves the shop together, just like the Marines, leave no man behind. You are the best crew that I have ever had. You have proved to me that you can get things done, and well when I'm not around. God bless you all, now lets go feed those hungry men out there. They all clapped for Ray and started out the doors with tray's in their hands.

Ray went and changed and then went back out on the floor in his tuxedo as if nothing happened. Ray's hands and ears still burned. Tony Larussa came up and shook Ray's hand and thanked him for a really nice set up. Ray thanked him and said wel it's kind of like the same, we both have our team that makes everything fall into place. Yes, you are right, then Tony shook Ray's ahnds again and walked off to join the others. Ray rubbed his hands together again to keep the circulation going, he was glad that Gail wasn't here, she would make him go to the hospital. It was going to be a long night.

Captain Lane walked up to Ray and shook his hand. "How is everything going Ray?" Just fine now, about an hour ago, I was almost a people pop, I'm talking frozen to the bone. Terry called Bob over so Ray didn't have to repeat it twice. Ray then told them abouthearing someone closing the freezer door, then he went around to see who was still there. When he opened the freezer someone pushed him in and locked the door with a sharping steel. Ray told them that he was in there for fifteen to twenty minutes until Adam got him out. Okay said Terry, no more freezer visits and no one leaves without the other, they all could be in danger. I have already had a meting with my staff and we will watch each others backs. I'm just glad Gail's not here to see my ears.

Well don't start off on the wrong foot by keeping things from her whatever it is, said Debbie Lane, the Captains wife, and with her another lovely lady. Ray Bertolli, I'd like for you to meet my wife Debbie and Bob's wife Patricia Nichols. Pleased to meet you laldies, I hope everything will be to your liking. With that said, Ray had Adam show them to their chairs, right next to Pujols nd his wife.Adam introduced them to each other and when Terry sat down, he told Bob. Man, Marshall and Womack are going to have a fit over this one. I better bring them something or I'm on the shit list for a long time. Ray was walking by their table when Terry asked him, Ray, do you or does anyone in your family have a clue as to who could be doing this? My Uncles have some suspitions, but need more time and information. I just don't know Terry, I need to get over to the reception table, have a great evening.

About the time that they were bringing out the Entree's, Terry's phone rang, he thought about ignoring it but then thought better of it. He wished he would have turned it off. It was only eight-thirty.

Chapter 37

Marshall and Womack got back to the station, re-checked the man his rights, but he still wouldn't talk, so back to the cell for him. He could get his one phone call in the morning. Mark called the two officers that they left at the scene. "Everything is just fine here, we double checked the building again and made sure that their house was locked up tighter than a drum. Who ever would try and get into that house tonight would be crazy. "With those two Bertolli brothers, I wouldn't want to go in there tonight" Okay, said Mark keep me posted of anything Mark said as he hung up the phone.

Mark then called Captain Lane. "This had better be important Marshall, Terry said with a smile."Well that all depends on important like, hello how are you? "OR" guess what we got, a shooter taking shots at the Bertolli house about an hour ago and we have one of them in our cell here right now. Terry jumped up and waved for Bob to follow. Do you know who it is? Not yet all he wants to do is talk to his lawyer, he keeps saying, so he just dummy'd up right from the beginning. We locked him up and told him he would get his call in the morning. Was anyone hurt, asked Terry? No sir, just a little shaken up. Joelina was the only one in the upstairs bedroom when the bullet went through her window. I'm going to check on her in the afternoon tomorrow. I have asked the Bertolli brothers to come down for a line up tomorrow at ten a.m. The look in their eyes said that they just wanted to take him and take care of things tonight on their terms, I have no doubt about that, Dominic wanted to go out to the car and beat it out of him. I had a cruiser bring him down here where he would be safe from those Bertolli brothers.

Well you're not the only one with troubles tonight Mark, Terry said. "Someone tried to freeze Mr. Ray Bertolli to death, had his staff not as been so quick, he would be dead by now."Did you catch the guy, said Mark? No, it was at the catering warehouse, while he was finishing up on the ice carving for tonight. "Well it looks like one for Marshall and Womack and zero for Lane and Nichols, laughed Mark and Dave. You think so huh. "Hey Bob, tell smartass here who we are sitting next to. Bob replied, Pojols and his wife." No way man, hey I was just kidding about that one and zero thing, you guys rule. Did you get us any autographs yet? Goodbye Marshall, see you at seven a.m. sharp. Yes Captain, but what about the.....hello....hello? The phone just went dead. That was just cold, to rub our noses in it because we're not there."We better get something out of this or there will be hell to pay."Don't tell them that I said that, Mark said? Womack couldn't stop laughing and shaking his head.

Marshall walked back to the holding cell and asked Mr. John Doe if he had changed his mind and wanted to talk, he just smiled and said, I will talk to my attorney. Well he won't be here until after one tomorrow afternoon, and the Bertolli brothers are coming to see you in a line up at ten in the morning. Personally, I'd be talking with God tonight and getting right with the Lord, because they'll see you before your lawyer will. "You don't scare me!" I"m not trying to, I'm just letting you know what's going to happen in the morning." Still don't want to talk? Okay, Mark said as he was walking back down the hall, sure hope those brothers can't break through that two way glass mirror, I don't think that I could hold them back, no, not at all. Mark went whistling all the way down the hall. The prisoner was a little paler now.

Chapter 38

Gail had locked up and was on her way up the stairs to bed when a weird feeling came over her. She felt like something was wrong, but couldn't pin point what it was. She went over and checked the windows and doors, they were locked as before. Well, it wasn't that, it must be someone calling out to her, or something else, she just didn't know, but it was something she could feel it. Her stomach was rolling.

Gail woke up bright and early after not much sleep, but she still felt it in the morning, she couldn't stop herself, she called Steven. "Hello mother, how are you, and why are you calling so early for, is something wrong?" I just have this feeling that something is just not right so I called to check on you first, since you have the dangerous job of being a police officer, are you okay? "Yes Mom, I'm fine and everything is okay in Hickory Grove as of six o'clock this morning." Only a couple of DUI's and a couple of domestic calls, other than that everything is just fine, nothing dangerous all night, in fact, I plan on sleeping until three or four today. "Well I'm glad that your fine, and our town is fine also." You get some sleep and I'll talk to you later. I love you. I love you too Ma, bye. Good bye son.

Gail then called Katie, oh she wasn't up yet. "Good morning sweetheart, it's Mom, are you okay?" "Mom, are you having one of your freaky something's wrong thing again?" Is that the reason for the early wakeup call? Yes dear, are you okay? "I'm fine Mom, but I'm going back to bed, see you on Tuesday, love you Mom. Good bye Katie, I'm sorry that I woke you up. That's alright Mom, I love you. I love you too baby. Gail didn't want to call Ray, she knew he probably worked late last night with the Cardinal's party. She would wait and call him from the hospital or once she got into her office. Gail showered and dressed and then went off to do her hospital rounds before going to the office.

When Gail got to the hospital, she found out that Mr. Kadell was back in the hospital. Dr. Yang had admitted him last night. Gail was at the second floor nurses station talking to Margie, and asked her how Ms. Boden was behaving. "Butter would not melt in her mouth, she has been the model patient since you had that talk with her." Thank you so much. "Well you are quite welcome; no one should be treated that way." "What's going on with Mr. Kadell in 202 B?" Margie stated that they brought him in complaining off swollen testicles and pain in his pelvic and groin area, they drew labs on him last night, and they are on his chart. We'll I'm of to see him now, thank you Margie. Thank you Dr. McDougal, and you have a nice day.

Gail reached Mr.Kadell's room but he was sleeping, she would come back in a little while. Gail went in to see Mrs. Youngblood. Good morning doctor, how are you? I'm fine, and how are you feeling this morning? Better, still congested, but it's starting to come up and out. Good said Gail, lets take a look up your nose and in your ears first. Yes you still have a lot of congestion in your sinuses, lets listen to your back and chest. Take in a deep breath, again, again, one more time, this time take in a real deep breath, good job. Sherry started coughing and got up some of the green monster as she calls it. Now, if I send you home with a nebulizer machine and medications, do you promise me that you will take the medications and use the machine four times a day? "Oh yes doctor, said Sherry, I promise, I want to go home so bad, I miss my family. You know that you can't have a lot of people in and out all the time or you will end up right back here in this bed, Gail told her. I will stay in my bed at home until I am well.

My husband Denny, already told the kids, that they can't bring themselves or my grandchildren over until we get the okay from you. "Okay then, we have a deal. The nurse will be in with your discharge papers and instructions for when you get home, so probably after breakfast you can call your family to come and pick you up. "You be careful and I'll need to see you in one week, so call my office and set up an appointment." I'll see you Sherry. Goodbye and thank you Dr. McDougal.

Gail then went in to see Ms. Boden, she was awake also. "How are you today Ms. Boden? I'm very well doctor and you? I'm fine thank you. "Do you know when I will be able to get out of here, Cynthia asked?" Well let's listen to your heart and see how you are doing this morning. Gail listened in four different places for about a minute. It sounds wonderful, the best it's been in a long time. Let's take your pulse and blood pressure and see how it's doing today. Blood pressure is 138/84, really good for you, pulse rate is 92, not the best, but not bad either. "Do you feel like going home today?" Yes, please, that would be awesome, thank you Dr. McDougal. You are welcome, you can call your family and have them pick you up after breakfast and the nurse brings down your discharge papers. Call my office and set up an appointment for next week or two, sometime after you get home, I'll see you then, and good luck. Thank you doctor. Your very welcome Ms. Boden.

As Gail walked down the hall, she had her doubts about Ms. Boden keeping her blood pressure down; she hoped for her own good that she would, she would see next week.

Gail walked in to see Mr. Kadell, he was still sleeping but, she picked up his wrist to take his pulse. It was 102, she was getting ready to take his blood pressure when He said, "I just can't seem to stay away from you, can I Sweet Pea?" Have you missed me Doc? Gail smiled and told him that she always misses him. By the looks of that ring, I don't think that I have a chance now, do I? I'm afraid not Gary, I'm already spoken for. "Do you think, I could take him?" Not in the condition that you're in. Gail took his blood pressure it was 180/98 not good at all. Well I think I'm going to put you on some Lasix 40 mg. twice a day for ten days, you'll be in here most of those days, I'm also going to have them put in a catheter, so I can keep track of how much water we can get off of you in that amount of time. I want you to have a prostate check while you're here also. Have you ever had one done before, asked Gail? No Doc, I try and stay away from tests, as you well know. Yes, I know, but you need to get ready because I'm putting you through the mill for your own good. I'm going to find out what's wrong with you. "Your heart has been doing fine so, I think I'm going to have a Urologist look at you maybe tomorrow, so be ready." They will also be doing more blood work. You take care and I'll see you in the morning. Good bye Doc, and thanks for taking the time for me. "You know I can't say no to you, Gail said with a smile." You behave yourself, and leave these poor nurses alone. "I can't control those women, they know a good thing when they see it." Gail turned and gave Gary a stern look. I'll be good I promise, said Gary.

Gail made it to the office with ten minutes to spare, she wanted to call Ray but, all four of her exam rooms were full. She would try at lunch time if she could, or just see him at his parents' house later.

Chapter 39

Ray woke up in a sweat, he was thinking that maybe he's not over that freezer thing yet, he dreamed about it all night long. Maybe, it will take a little time. He tried to go back to sleep but couldn't, so he got up and put the coffee on. He was going to call Gail, but when he looked at the clock, he knew that she would be with patients now, he might try later or just see her at his parents' house later. Ray was off today, the whole day; it was nice for a change. Ray thought to himself, I wonder what Mama's fixing for dinner tonight. Whatever it was it would be awesome. His mother sure knew how to cook! Ray would tell Gail and his parents at the same time about what had happened last night. Ray walked around the house and cleaned up a little just in case he could get Gail to stay the night. He hoped that she would. It's like he misses her the minute she's gone. "Yes, he loved this woman dearly."

Ray decided to catch up on some paper work when the phone rang, it was his uncle. "Hello Uncle Dominic, how are you this morning?" I'm fine Ray, I need you and Roberto to meet Vincent, myself and your father down at the police station on Market street at ten o'clock sharp. Why? "What's going on Uncle Dominic?" Just be there, I'll call Roberto also, I'll talk to you then, and before Ray could say another word, Dominic had hung up. It was nine-fifteen already, so he took his coffee upstairs with him to shower and get dressed. What on earth could be going on for everyone to be at the police station this morning? Maybe they heard about what happened to him and they have a suspect in custody, if so Captain Lane works fast to catch the bad guys. Ray had one more cup of coffee and then left for the station. Please let this day be good Lord!

Roberto was at the Zoo already when his Uncle Dominic called him. "What do you mean, meet everyone at the police station by ten?" I am at work Uncle Dominic, it's hard for me to leave right now. "I have a leopard almost ready to give birth and I need to be here when that happens. "You need to be with your Papa!" Ten o'clock, be there, and then he hung up. "Was something wrong with Papa again?" Roberto would have to tell his staff to page him, and that he'll be back as soon as possible.

Chapter 42

Captain Lane and Detective Bob Nichols were waiting for Marshall and Womack to come back in after a night of hell. When they got there they looked like they had been run over. "What's wrong boy's didn't you get any sleep last night? Well boss, it's kind of hard to do when you work straight midnight's or twelve hour shift's for two weeks or more, I think I lost track, how about you Dave, what do you think? Womack just said let's get this over so we can go to bed. Here maybe this will help you to have sweet dreams as Terry threw them both a baseball, and it was signed by the whole team. Thanks captain, I knew that you would pull through for us. Mark looked at Dave and they both started laughing.

Terry said okay, let's go talk to your John Doe, that nobody knows, and see if he wants to talk to us now or before the Bertolli brothers and sons get here and try to kill him. You know Captain, I told him the same thing last night. When they got to the man's cell, he was awake and starring at the floor. "What's the matter, couldn't sleep?" Are you ready to talk yet? "Yes, when my attorney gets here." Okay, last chance." They all walked back together and started their de-briefing from the night before. "Have you talked to the officers who took your place yet this morning Marshall?" Yes, they said that the rest of the night was peaceful, no more problems. Now that it's light out, CSI is going over there and collect blood samples and whatever else they can pick up on. We roped it all off last night and Chappel said that no one has been over there, they will stay there until CSI is finished.

About that time Terry saw the Bertolli brothers walking up the stairs at the station. Michael, said Dominic, before we get in here if you think that you know him, do not say anything, it's a family matter and we will take care of things our way. Yes, I don't like it, putting that lunatic back out there on the street, so he can shoot at my house again, I don't like it. Mark and Dave walked up to meet them. Good morning gentlemen, can I get you some coffee, Mark said? Yes, please, that would be nice said Michael. Have a seat here and I'll be right back. Do you need sugar or cream for your coffee? No Mark, we all drink ours just black, thank you, said Michael. Mark would have to try and remember that, you never know when it might come in handy.

Mark came back with the coffee and Captain Lane was with him. Captain Lane, this is Michael, Vincent and Dominic Bertolli, Terry shook each ones hands as they were introduced. How are you gentlemen doing this morning Terry said? When your sons get here, we will do this all at once, before this man talks to his attorney. There is also some other news that your son Ray has to tell you about last night also. Ah, here they come now.

Ray met Roberto in the parking lot at the same time. "So Ray, what's going on here, do you know what it is?" Yes, part of it, but they say that there is more news to tell, so here I am. "Are you off today Roberto?" No, I had to leave just when my leopard was going into labor, it could take a couple of day's or a couple of hours. When they got to the doors, everyone else was already there it looked like. Ray looked at Roberto and said, well let's go and join the party.

Ray and Roberto was introduced to everyone and given coffee as well. Mark took them to a conference room so they could talk. When everyone was seated, Terry started with what had happened to Ray last night. Everyone looked at Ray and Michael said, are you alright my son? I'm fine now Papa, my fingers and ears still sting a little but, I'm fine. Mark then filled in Ray and Roberto about what had happened at their fathers house. Everyone seemed like they were in shock or something until Vincent said, "we want to see this man now please." the room was deadly quiet. Bob and Dave were in the room also when Dave spoke up and said, "Now you realize that this man did not work alone." I got two shots fired off and I am 100% sure that I hit him, but he had a car around the corner and got away while I was cuffing this man that you are about to see. "We just want to see this person, then we'll know more, said Dominic.

Mark lead the Bertolli brothers into a room with a large glass two way mirror. Okay, we will have six to seven people come out in the lineup, If you think that you know him, don't hesitate to speak up, if you want a closer look just tell me which number and they will bring him closer. "Are you ready?" Okay, let's bring them out. Mark pressed a button and seven different men walked out in a straight row and told to turn forward. As they were looking at them, Mark could see no reaction on their faces, except for Roberto. "Do you see someone you know Roberto, asked Mark?" Number five looks familiar to me but, I just don't know. Mark pushed the button and said, number five, please step forward and turn to you right. Does anyone else know anyone or someone who you might have met in your store Michael? They all , but shook their heads no. except Roberto. Take another look at him Roberto, Mark said as he pushed the button. Number five, turn forward please. Roberto said that he just didn't know who he was or where he could have seen him before. Okay, lets go back into the conference room, said Dave. Mark pushed the button and then dismissed the line-up.

Back in the confrence room Terry, Dave, Mark and Bob stayed in a connecting room to see if they could hear anything from there men, nothing was said at all for five minutes. Terry went in and told them that they could all leave now, but this man will probably be turned loose when his lawyer got there. He had no gun residue on him and his finger prints were not on the gun, so we have nothing to hold him on. I'm sorry said Roberto, do you have a card that I could call you if I can remember anything? Yes, Terry said, here is my card and you can call anytime day or night. I'm sorry he said to his Papa and Uncles. It's okay Roberto, we will watch each other's back with the help of these fine men said Michael.

Everyone but Ray left, and he told Terry that he could tell that no one knew him. I'll be there tonight for dinner, when we announce our engagement. We all need some good news.

Chapter 42

After Roberto left for work, Sonny came up from the basement, where he had slept. The children were still upstairs getting ready for school. Lucinda asked Sonny if he would like some breakfast before he left for the airport. No he replied, he would pick up something. You know I heard you and Roberto last night arguing over me. "Why do you let him talk to you like that Lucinda?" He has no right to treat you like shit, and he calls me a shit bumm! Roberto is just under a lot of pressure now with work and everything else going on with his family, and his father being sick. Sonny just kind of giggled at that remark. Sonny then slammed his fist down on the table, and for the first time, she was afraid of her brother. I don't care, it makes no difference to me, you should never let him speak to you like that, he treats you like shit and he can go to hell. "Sonny I think that you need to leave now, I don't want the children upset. I'll go as soon as I take a shower and get the fifteen hundred dollars, so have it ready for me when I get done. Lucinda thought back to the night before when She asked Roberto if it was okay to give Sonny the money.

I was talking to my brother and he wants us to loan him fifteen hundred dollars, is that alright? When in the hell is he ever going to get a job, and stop being such a shit bumm? We have the money, why can't I help out my brother? You do whatever the hell you want, send it to him, then Roberto went back to bed.

As Lucinda was counting out the money, she thought to herself, he was her brother and he has lots of problems, but she didn't want him back in their house again. Lucinda went up the stairs to help her children get ready for school. Roberto ahd already taken Lucus blood sugar, she would take it again at four when he got off of the bus. Maybe she would go out for a walk today, they say that the weather was going to be great. As she walked passed the bathroom Lucinda saw the door slightly opened. When she looked down, she saw some pieces of towel torn into strips, and covered in blood lying next to his clothes.Sonny turned off the shower and Lucinda walked into her bedroom. What was going on with Sonny, was he hurt bad? She knew better than to say anything about it, he would go ballistic if she did.

Lucinda hurried the children, and got Sonny's money as sooon as she could. Come on chidren, lets get breakfast and then off to school. "Sonny, are you sure that you don't want some breakfast?" How many times do I have to tell you, you stupid bitch, just give me my money and I'l be gone so your asshole of a husband can shut up about his loser brother-in-law. "Sonny, you will watch what you say in this house and in front of my children, said Lucinda.Sonny came out of the bathroom with his dirty clothes in a bag; he looked at Lucinda and just shook his head, he then took his clothes out to his rental car. Sonny thought that he was glad that the car was not in his name, but an alias and he will leave it at the airport. He did have some unfinished buisness to do before his flight took off at ten o'clock this evening. It shouldn't take long and he would still get paid no matter which Bertolli went down. Sonny decided to change the plan now that Eduardo Gianti was in jail. "Come on Lucinda, lets go I need that money today, now, not next week. I'm in a hurry to get out of this God forsaking place." Okay Sonny stop yelling at me, cried Lucinda! You should be used to it by now, with that husband of yours. Lucinda gave the money to her brother and said, you are no longer welcome in my home, I would like for you to leave now. "Thank you sis, and remember that you can alway's come back home to Sicily should something happen between you and your hot shot Roberto. Lucina said, may you have a safe flight home, but don't ever come to my doorstep ever again.

Whatever, like that would break my heart, see ya, then out the door he went.

When he left, Lucinda locked every door and window, she would make-up with Roberto tonight for defending her brother, and not standing along her husband when he needed her too. After going up the stairs to throw a load of towls into the laundry, Lucinda found a piece of bloody towel, if he only twisted his knee why would there be so much blood, he also shaved off his mustache and trimmed his hair, it was all over the place. What did Sonny do last night Lucinda wondered.

Yes, it was a good thing that Roberto wasn't here and saw the mess that Sonny left, Roberto would have told Sonny to go back up those stairs and clean up his mess. He would have also blackend his eye for speaking to Lucinda that way, and in front of the children. Roberto would have also want an explination as to why there was so much blood for a twisted knee. "Mom, were ready for school." I'll be right down, said Lucinda. Sony could not get on that plane fast enough for Roberto, and she felt for once the same way. "What was Sonny up to?" Whatever it was, It was evil, she could feel it. Lucinda finished in the bathroom and took the trash down to the trash can in the garage, she didn't want anyone to see it.

Sonny left with the cash and headed to the airport to get his ticket, that way later he wouldn't have to stand in line. Eduardo would have to fend for himself, that was the plan, we take care of ourselves if something went wrong, and it seemed that everything went wrong. Two missed chances, and still the job not done. He felt funny without his mustache, but he would grow it back when he got home. After pre-checking in at Lambert Airport, he might just make a trip to the Zoo. He had never hunted in a zoo before."Yes Sonny thought, plans have been changed, no one talks to his sister like that and gets away with it.

Lucinda would be fine; she would come back to Sicily with the children. She could start out new again, people do it all the time Sonny thought. Lucinda would forget about Roberto, and be back home with Mama and himself. Things alway's found a way of working out, they alway's did, thats why he had to go to the Zoo tonight, before his flight home.

Chapter 43

Gail was with her last patient before she knew it. She had worked right through lunch hour. She never got the chance to call Ray all day, she was seeing patients that had to be seen from her time away from the office. When Gail went back into her office after her last patient, her office manager came in and wanted to talk about vacations and holiday's coming up before they new it.

Pat, how are you? I know we said hello this morning, but that's been it all day. I know, said Pat, and I have been waiting all day to get a close up of that ring on your finger. We are all dying to see it. With that said, Gail held out her hand and let Pat see the ring. "I dont think that I have ever seen anything so beautiful in my life; did Ray pick it out himself?" That's the beauty of it, yes he did. Didn't he do a wonderful job? It's extremely awesome, replied Pat. Does he have any brothers or uncles that are single? Gail laughed and said, he has only one brother, who is married, but he does have two uncles that are single and in town right now from Sicily. "Well fix me up Dr. McDougal; I'm game if they are." They laughed again as the other staff members came in to see Gail's ring. They couldn't believe that Ray picked it out on his own. Did he go to Jared's? "Yes, he really did do it on his own, he said the blue diamonds matched my eyes, as she flutterd her eye lashes. Everyone at the same time said, Awe!

After everyone left to go home, Gail got the chance to call Ray. "Hi baby, hows my favorite girl?" Starving, what time do you need me to meet you and where, your house or your parents? Why don't you just come by here and we can only take one car to my Mom and Pop's. Would that work for you? That sound's great, what time. How does six-thirty sound, then we can be at the folks house by seven? That sound's fine babe, I'll see you in a half an hour then, I love you. I love you too Kiddo; see you when you get here. Gail finished charting for the day then to freshen up. She had worn her favorite blue dress under her Doctor's coat, and was glad to see that she didn't get it dirty. Gail freshened up her make-up and let her hair fall down her back, she would need a trim soon. Gail still looked out the peep hole before going out to the elevators, she was still a little nervous about walking out alone to the parking garage. She looked around and saw no one so she got into her car and locked the doors. Gail took the fastest route to Ray's house by taking side streets. Route 40 was under constuction, so that way meant a very long line of traffic.

When Gail got to Ray's, he was standing in the door, waiting for her. "Hello babe, I sure have missed you." Ray, it's only been two days, she smiled. Well, it semed like a life time for me. Do we need to leave right now, or can I bring some things inside? "Your the one who said that you were starving?" I really only need to to put my overnight case, and some clothes in the house, do you mind if I stay the night? "I'm pretty sure that I wont mind at all, in fact I hoped you would." Gail said that she needed to use the restroom first, she was back in about ten minutes and said, okay let's go. Ray asked her if she alway's took this long of a time in the bathroom just to freshen up, because they would need two bathrooms. My house has two and a half, if you have forgotten. I am really hungry for some reason. Ray asked her if she had eaten lunch, and Gail replied no that she hadn't, she worked right through the lunch hour.

Gail got into Ray's Cadillac DeVille; made sure that she was strapped in and ready to go, and then they were off. While driving Ray started to tell Gail about the freezer incident, and what happened at his parents house last night. "Oh my God Raymond are you alright, do you need me to look at your ears and fingers?" No honey, really I'm just fine. I have to admit it did scare me a little bit more than I can say, the part of never seeing you was the worst part "Ray, pull over, please pull the car over." Are you going to be sick honey? No, just please pull over. Ray pulled over and put the car in park. Gail unlocked her seatbelt and then grabbed onto Ray like she was never going to let him go. "Sweetheart, don't cry, I'm fine and your never going to have to worry about me at work anymore." I made a new rule that everyone leaves together, so that this can't happen to anyone again. "I love you baby, please don't cry anymore." There is something else, not to me babe, as Gail started to shake again, someone shot the upstairs bedroom window out at my parent's house last night. No one was hurt but, Joelina was upstairs when it happened in her bedroom. "Are you alright Gail?" Yes, I think so she said as she dug for some tissues in her purse. My stomach is just rolling, it must be nerves. I was just overcome for a moment, she put her seatbelt back on and they continued on their way to Ray's parents house. Gail just starred out the window, life is too short she thought, she wanted to get married right away. Gail didn't want to miss out on one moment with him anymore.

Ray, do they know yet, who is doing this, who is the man in custody, does anyone know him at all?"

They're working on it babe, but as of yet no one knows who he is, not only that but, it wasn't his fingerprints on the rifle, so after twenty-four hours they may have to let him go. Roberto said that he looked kind of familiar to him, but couldn't place him right now. "You mean to tell me that they have let him out?" Yes, we can only hope that nothing will happen again. What about the man that was shot? We have no idea who that was. They were pulling into his parents driveway and Ray said that they would talk more on the way home. Now, he just wanted to celebrate with his fiance'.

Chapter 44

Roberto stopped back at the house before going back to the zoo. He would eat lunch at home today and try to talk to his wife. When he pulled up Lucinda was in the flowerbeds. When he walked up to her it startled her, she had her I-POD on and didn't hear him drive up. She got up slowley and then reached out to hold her husband, he held her also. "I hate arguing Lucinda, I'm sorry." I'm sorry too Roberto, but I want to say even more than that, you were right about my brother Sonny. Sweetheart; it's okay to give him the money if he really needs it, then by all means give it to him, it won't hurt our marraige, said Roberto. I will make it up to you, I promise. There's nothing to make up for Lucinda; I love you and our family no matter what, what we share as a family can't be torn down over money. I gave Sonny the money already Roberto, but I also told him to never come to our house again.

Roberto, I think Sonny is up to no good. He was here this morning when you left for work, he was down in the basement. I let him in last night because he said that he had no place to sleep. You could have told me that honey, said Roberto. "When he came up the stairs, he wanted to take a shower, get the money and leave." I asked him if he wanted some breakfast and he started screaming at me about you. He had heard us last night and this morning and was upset by your tone of voice to me, he said. When he went up the stairs, he was limping, when I asked him what happened to him, he said that he twisted his knee on the sidewalk, and for me to just shut up and get his money ready for him after he showered. It worry's me what he has been up to, I feel it is an evil thing. He was very angry when he left, slamming his fist down on the table in front of our children. That was when I told him to leave and never come to our house again. He said that he will be leaving Lambert airport at ten o'clock tonight for Sicily. Yes Lucinda, he better be on that plane if he knows what's good for him, said Roberto, kissing the tears away.

Now that Roberto and Lucinda had made up (twice), Roberto was going back to the zoo to check out his mama and baby leopards. I may not be home tonight, he had told Lucinda, it all depends on Sahara's labor. I'll call you if I stay at the zoo. I'll be here waiting for you sweetheart. "Please be careful, taking babies away from their mothers is a dangerous situation, no matter human or animal" "I'll be fine, I've done this before remember?"

Roberto was singing to himself and feeling really good on the ride to the zoo, he was thinking about Lucinda and their children, he was surely blessed. All of a sudden he pulled over and stopped the car. A cold sweat broke out and trickeled down his forehead. Roberto did know this man; he used to hang around with Sonny back in Sicily. That's where he had seen him before.

Roberto pulled out Captain Lane's phone number and dialed his cell phone. "Captain Lane, how can I help you?" Captain Lane, this is Roberto Bertolli, we spoke this morning? "Yes, how are you Roberto?" I'm afraid not so well, I remember where I saw this man at the station this morning. His name is Eduardo Gianti, and he is a friend of my brother-in-law, Sonny. I'm terrified for my wife and children. Lucinda had a quarrel with Sonny this morning and told him to never come back to our home. I didn't know that he was even in the States until a little bit ago. Captain, please, do you have anyone who could stay with my wife and children? My wife said that Sonny was limping and said that he just twisted his knee, but after he left the house, Lucinda went up and found some bloody towell strips hidden under some other towels. I'm afraid that Sonny is the man that got shot and then got away. "Have you released Eduardo yet sir?" I'm afraid that we could only hold him for so long, his prints wern't on the gun that was fired into your father's home, but I bet I know now who's is. I will run them through Interpoll, has Sonny been arrested in Sicily before Roberto? Yes, many times said Roberto. Alright, I'll send someone over to your house, what is your address?, Roberto gave it to him. Now, said Terry, call your wife and tell her that my men are going over there and why. Roberto, you need to watch out for yourself, he might come after you. I will sir, but I'm not worried about me only my family, I will call my wife now, the children should be home from school by now, please keep them all safe. Roberto called Lucinda and let her know what was going on and to watch for the policemen to come to the door and to not let the children out of the house.

Chapter 45

Ray and Gail got to his parents house just in time to smell the chicken parmesan coming out of the oven, Christina had also made French bread, a salad and German chocolate cake, all of Ray's favorites. Gail, Raymond, please come in and take a seat, Michael hugged and kissed both of them. We are pleased to have you here in our home, please sit down you are right on time. "I hope you are hungry, cried Christina from the kitchen door as it opened. We are famished said Gail. I missed lunch today; I had too many patients to catch up on. Talking will come after the meal tonight then I think, said Michael. When they all sat down, Dominic said that it was his turn to say the blessing, everyone bowed their heads. "Dear heavenly father, bless this family and friends, thank you for this wonderful meal that Christina has made from her heart. Keep us all safe Lord, in Jesus name Amen. Amen! Let's eat, said Raymond.

Everyone was eating and there wasn't much talking at first, but when everyone was getting full, they started to talk a little. Gail was in heaven, these were all of her favorites also. Christina, you have outdone yourself tonight said Gail stuffing another piece of bread down. "Thank you so very much Gail, but don't you think it's time to start calling me Mama?" Oh, that would be so wonderful, you have no idea what an honor that would be for me after loseing my parents. "You must also call me Papa, said Michael." Gail got tears in her eyes, and for the first time in a long time, she felt a warm home presence. Only someone who has lost his or her parents, can one truly understand.

Joelina started clearing the table when the door bell rang. Vincent went to answer it. It was Mark coming to pick up Joelina for a date. Mark had called earlier in the day to ask Joelina if she would like to go to a movie, she said yes. Please, said Gail, you go on, I'll help to finish up the dishes. Are you sure Gail? Yes, now go, have fun but, first I have something to show you all. Gail looked over to Ray and said, "Ray, your on!" Mama, Papa and the rest of my wonderful family gathered here tonight, Gail has agreed to marry me, I am the luckiest man in the world. "Oh my, what a wonderful gift for all of us tonight, cried Christina." We already love you. Gail showed them all her ring. It's so beautiful, Ray, did you pick this out by yourself said Joelina, and did you go to Jared's? With that everyone started laughing. Jared's is a diamond store in St. Louis. "Yes, I did, nothing is too good for my lady as he looked at Gail and smiled. While the lady's were enjoying Gails ring, Michael pulled Raymond aside and said, son I know that you loved Vanessa, but life goes on and you have made a wise choice in Gail, be happy Ray, you deserve it. "Thank you Papa, I will, Gail makes me very happy and she is the only girl for me." Ray looked around and even the uncles had tears in their eyes. Mark was standing by the door just smiling. Dominic walked up to him and said; "Someday I hope that you find a woman to be as happy with as these two here tonight." I think I'm working on that now sir, as he starred at Joelina with stars in his eyes. Joelina asked Mark if he was ready to go, and he said yes that he was and for her to grab a sweater, it's getting a little chilly out tonight. Congatulations to you both Mark said as he took Jolina out the door. They were going to see a movie with Dave and his wife Jennifer, which one they had yet to decide.

After the dishes were done and everyone was seated around the table for cake and coffee, did Ray tell them that he had let Gail know about what happened the last couple of nights. "I feel so frightend for all of you, please be careful of your suroundings at all times, Gail said. I wouldn't want to lose any of you now that I have you as my family and love you so much. "So Gail, not to change the subject but when is the big day, asked Dominic?" "Well we haven't set a date as of yet." If it was up to me it would be tomorrow, Ray said. Maybe not tomorrow but soon, I need to talk with my children about everything. We are taking them to dinner next Wednesday. So, your daughter will be home for a while, yes? asked Christina. Yes she will be here for two weeks, but four of those day's she'll be at the fashion show at the America Center. "Well she does know how to design clothes, Joelina said that she is almost afraid to wear the dress that Katie made her, it is so pretty. Gail stood up and said, let's go get that cake, I'm still hungry, she went into the kitchen to help bring out the cake and coffee and the dishes. Christina looked at Gail and smiled. All had not been told tonight, but soon I'm sure thought Christina, all in good time.

Chapter 46

Captain Lane called in Bob, Mark and Dave into the statiom immediatly. Men we have a positive Match for our John Doe, which we let that son-of-a-bitch walk right out of here this morning. His name is Eduardo Gianti from Sicily, and he's friends with Roberto Bertolli's wife Lucinda's brother Sonny. He has a lot of priors from Sicily and they sent over his fingerprints, which match the ones on the rifle from the shooting at the home of Michael Bertolli. Roberto has also told me that Sonny was at his house this morning when he left for work, Roberto idn't even know that he was here. Sonny was in the basement, and didn't come up until Roberto left for work this morning.

When Roberto left for work, he noticed a gray car on the side of the street, he just thought the neighbors had company. Roberto's wife told him just an hour ago that Sonny was driving it. As of now, I have Blackorby and Summers on watch inside of Roberto's house to watch over his wife and children. Lucinda said that when he left this morning that Sonny was very angry when he left their house this morning. He was screaming at Lucinda in front of the children and she told him to never come back to their home again.I'm hoping that he does come back so we cane nail the bastard while he's still in the States. He is suppose to have a ticket for the ten o'clock tonight back to Sicily, if so he's using an alias. Lucinda also said that he shaved his mustache off and cut his hair to try and change his apperance. Cunningham and Chappel are still outside Michael Bertolli's house. Ray and Dr. McDougal are there also. "Yes, I just saw them when I picked up Joelina." We were on our way to see a movie when you called us in, Mark said. Joelina and Jennifer are in the lobby now. "Well, get those ladies home, I have a bad feeling about tonight." Okay Captain, we'll be right back after we get the girls home. "Good, Bob and I will try and think of a way to bring them out, or hunt them down while your gone. Dave and Mark left to take the girls home.

Sonny was on his way to the zoo when he got a call on his cell phone. "Who could that be?" Hello, this is Sonny." Well hello Sonny, this is Eduardo; not enough evidence to hold me on so they had to cut me loose, where are you Sonny, can you pick me up? I was just on my way to the zoo to do a little night hunting, the two legged kind, why, do you want to go? Yeah, sure said Eduardo, pick me up at Tenth and Market streets, I'll be on the corner. Sonny hung up and thought wow, I still have someone on my side, now things should go easier with two people. Eduardo will have to take a later flight out, unless they didn't mess around for a long time and they could get there early. Trafic was good now maybe it would stay that way.

Ray and Gail were just saying their goodbyes when Ray's phone rang; they were going out the door. While Gail was getting in the car, Ray stopped and listened to Roberto explain what was happening. Things started to fall into place now, just like dominos. When Ray got into the car he told Gail that he needed to drop her off at his house, and that he would be back soon. He needed to go to the zoo and talk to Roberto. "I'm going with you Ray." "No you are not, I will not put you in harms way." Well, you don't have a choice because like it or not, I'm going, Gail told him."Fine, but you must stay with me at all times, deal? Deal she said. They barely spoke a word just starred down the highway. Both were afraid, of what they wern't sure of, but they would be together.

Roberto was in the stageing area; he knew that Sahara would have her cubs tonight, so he needed to be alert. He had lots of coffee to keep him and his assistant Daniel awake for hours. Sahara's cries were a good sign that she was in full labor now. Maybe an hour, maybe less, then they would have two new babies at the zoo. St. Louis was going to keep the girl and send the boy to the England zoo. The ultrasound showed one boy and one girl. Leopards stay with their mother for about two years, and then makes them go out on their own. Sahara's cries were getting stonger and louder, Roberto knew that in about ten minutes the babies would be here.

Sonny and Eduardo parked just outside the zoo's front entrance. It was dark out tonight , no moon or stars and it was hard to see, but that was fine they could move better undetected. In no time they were over the fence and would have to look for the cat cages, they had never been to this zoo before. That was fine, they had plenty of time to do what needed to be done. Even though it wasn't proven, Sonny knew that the Bertolli brothers had something to do with Eduardo's family member being killed four months ago. Sonny told Eduardo that this one was on the house, just because it was Roberto.

Chapter 47

      Mark and Joelina got into his car at Dave's house where he had left it to go to the movies. "Good bye Jennifer, it was very nice to meet you, and you too Dave, said Joelina." "I hope we will see each other soon said Jennifer, goodbye." Well a big monkey wrench was thrown into that. Mark kept apologizing, but Joelina told him not to worry. "You are going to protect my family, how could I be mad at you for that?" I just wish that we had more time together and get to know one another. "Mark, I feel like I already know you, you held me when I cried, you came to the Market to check me out, as Uncle Dominic pointed out, and you are so kind and loving." We will have time for another chance to get to know each other, that is if you still want to, do you? "Yes, most certainatly I do, does tomorrow sound good for you?" It sounds wonderful, said Joelina. They were pulling into her drive and neither wanted to say goodbye. Mark walked her up to the front door. "Would it be alright if I kissed you Joelina,

even thoigh we haven't really had our date yet?"
I think that would be just fine with me, I would
like it a lot.

Vincent walked to the door to see who was
out there, then just smiled and walked away.
Mark, you have already won over my family's
heart, and that is something no other man ahs
ever done, not that there have been that many.
I work in the store all the time, plus I"m finishing
up my Master's in buisnes. I don't have a lot of
time, soon I will take over the store and Papa
can rest with Mama. What about you Mark,
anymore schooling ahead for you? Yes, mark
replied I start a clas in criminal law and crime
scene investigators in five weeks. Mark's pager
went of before he could say anything else, it was
the Captain. I know you have to go, but could
you kiss me again, asked Joelina? No problem
at all, and with that Mark kissed Joelina long
and hard. Will that do until tomorrow? Yes, just
fine, goodnight Mark said Joelina as she floated
through the door.

When Joelina came in everyone was
smiling. "What are you al smiling about, it was
just a kiss. "So, he did kiss you, said Dominic
laughing. Uncle Dominic, if you don't stop teasing
me, I will have to hurt you in front of your brothers!
Then they all laughed, even Christina. "Why
are you back so soon dear, no good movies to

watch tonight?" "Oh ny gosh, I can't believe that I haven't told you yet with al the teasing going on." They think that Sonny Cabello is the person that Dave (officer Womack) shot in the leg two nights ago across the street. It seems that Eduardo Gianti is a relative to the person who was killed three or four months ago in Sicily. I'm not sure but, the police are now at Roberto's house with Lucinda and the children. Roberto is at the zoo with his leopards. Captain Lane just paged Mark again to call him. That's why I'm here early, I hope everything is okay.

Vincent went into the other room and called Ray."Raymond, do you know about Sonny and Eduardo?" Yes Uncle Vincent I do, thats why Gail and I are on our way to the zoo, they think that Roberto may be in trouble tonight. They also spotted the gray rental car, but then lost it on I-70, they must have pulled off of a side road or something. "Uncle Vincent, I need to know, is Eduardo related to the person who was killed three or so months ago?" Yes, Eduardo is his grandson. Thank you for telling me, I will let you know what happens at the zoo. Yes, thank you Raymond.

Vincent would not wait for an update, he pulled Dominic into the kitchen and told him what was happening. Without a sound, they went out the back door. They would call Michael from the car and let him know where they would be. "Dominic, we must stop this hatred tonight or it will go on and on through all of the children." I just hope we are in time to save Roberto. "It must stop now, Tonight!"

Chapter 48

Mark and Dave met up with Terry and Bob to go to the zoo. Terry sent a car to Maria and Erik's house, just in case, he wanted all areas covered. I hope the only thing happening at the zoo tonight is those cubs being born said Bob. Well I hope they're all asleep and everyone goes home safely, said Terry.

When they got to the entrance to the zoo, Mark noticed a car a little ways up the road a ways, pull up a little further Dave. I have a suspsition that this is the gray car we've been looking for, and yes, it's a rental. Mark got out and slowly moved up to the drivers side and shined a light inside. "There's no one here but there's blood on the drivers side seat and all down the inside of the door. He walked back to the others as they were getting out also. They were walking up to the gate when Captain Lane said, well guys, another long ass night so lock and load'em. Let's watch your asses and each others. "Dave, you and Mark start from the left, and Bob and I will start from the right, and meet in the center at the cages. Give us a sign if you see anything and be careful please!

Gail and Ray pulled up yo the side entrance. Ray parked in a no parking zone, he looked over at Gail and said, they can arrest me later, I'm going in here it is the quickest way into the cages. I need to be with my brother and fast. Ray asked Gail to stay in the car but he already knew the answer."No Ray, I will not. "We do this together; besides God forbid, someone might need me." They started in to where they knew the cages were, there they would find Roberto.

Vincent and Dominic pulled up behind the gray rental car. the first thing they saw was the unmarked police cruiser. Mark and his partners probably, that was a good sign. Vincent and Dominic did not know the zoo so it would be like finding a nedle in a hay stack. When Vincent called Michael from the car, they told him that they needed him to watch over Christina and Joelina. Michael then felt like he was doing something to help out his family, and he felt like their protector. Christina kept holding his hand and Joelina sat close to her father also, He did feel needed.

Roberto and Daniel was watching the birth of two leopard cubs, she had just finished giving birth to them and was trying to clean them up,

Sahara's crys were now a soft purr, and a low growl when ever Roberto or Daniel walked too close to the cage, as if to say leave my babies alone.Roberto was getting the tranquilizer gun ready to go into Saahra's hip. He pulled up and shot her in the left hip, they had to move fast because it wouldn't last for long. Sahara went down into a pile of straw away from the babies to where you could hardly see her at all. Roberto and Daniel went in and grabbed the cubs and started checking them out, weighing them, drawing their markings so as to tell them apart, and cleaning out their noses and mouths. Everything had to be charted down, they were working fast, the dart would wear off fast. They left the door to the cage open because they knew that they had to get the cubs back before she woke up. Daniel heard the cage door close and said to Roberto, man I hope that's not Sahara or were in big trouble. Roberto took the dart gun and went to check.

Chapter 49

Gail and Ray were getting closer to the leopard cages; they could hear voices but they couldn't tell who it was yet. When they rounded the corner, they saw Sonny with a gun pointed at Roberto. When Roberto came out to check the cages and Sahara, Sonny got the drop on him. Roberto still had the tranquilizer gun with him. "Sonny, please come out of that cage, it isn't safe. "Yeah, right asshole, why don't you scream at me like you did my sister lastnight and this morning?" Sonny, you need to come out of that cage, it's not safe for you in there, Eduardo, please come out of there, Roberto pleaded with them. "Hell no, this is probably the only way out of here and you can't stand to not be in control Sonny snarled at Roberto." Eduardo, come over here and see the monkeys in the cage. When Eduardo was walking up next to Sonny, Ray and Gail walked up next to Roberto and Daniel. "Well look what we got here said Sonny, more of the scumbag family that killed your grandfather

Eduardo, doesn't it feel good to know that now you can now avenge his death?"

Mark and Dave were coming up behind Sonny and Eduardo, as they got closer they were wondering why they were in the same cage as the leopard that was starting to move around a little. They silently got closer, but on the other side of the bars. It was at that time that Terry and Bob came up behind Roberto, Ray and Gail, but keeping a safe distance. "Sonny put down the gun and move very slowly out of the cage, you too Eduardo, said Terry."We can all work this out as gentlemen." "There were no gentlemen when they killed our mother and then raped and beat Dominic's girlfriend and then left her for dead said Vincent as they came up on the side of the cage. Dominic said,"you should die like the dogs that you are." What proof do you have that we have done anything wrong?" No one contacted us, or tried to come and see us to ask about your family, yet you come here to try and kill our brother Michael, who had never tried to hurt anyone. "Yes, we did try to kill Michael and would have but was interupted by his wife, I stole one of Lucus syringes without anyone knowing about it, but I forgot to pick up the top before I left. Then the chance for Joelina failed also, this is my chance now." Mark had a deep burning in his stomach when he heard Sonny say that about Joelina. "Revenge is sweet now because, I changed the plan myself, and let the luckey one be Roberto. "So you would rather your neices and nephew grow up without a father, said Ray." I really don't care as long as justice is done said Sonny. "You can't mean that Sonny, pleaded Gail.

You don't know how he screams at Lucinda; at least she had the grace to let me sleep in the basement last night. "Yes, and she also told you to never come back to our home didn't she, said Roberto?" I love my wife and children and I would die for them. "Good said Sonny, because that's what I have in mind for you, and your scum family. How was that freezer Ray, a little cold, ha ha ha! Please said Roberto, stop making loud noises and walk to the side of the cage by the door, do it now very slowly. "You still think that you can tell me what to do?" Those days are over, now it's my turn to tell you what to do Roberto. Sonny was in a deranged state of mind, everyone was pleading with him to get out of that cage.

Sahara was slowly starting to come out of sedation, she treid to stand up but was a little wobbly.Sonny kept on screaming at Roberto and how his sister will be so much better without him. Sonny, said Roberto, please walk over to the side door and get out of that cage, Eduardo, listen to me, run get out of there now, do it now, but it was too late. Sahara was standing now in a pounce mode, Eduardo finally saw her and moved a little closer to the door. Before he knew what hit him, Sahara jumped and and knocked Sonny to the ground, her giant fangs penetrating into his flesh, and in doing so he also knocked Eduardo to the ground, he jumped back up and was a little closer to the door. Roberto was getting the tranquilizer ready as fast as he could. Sonny was trying to shoot at the leopard, and in doing so, he fired off several rounds, one hitting Vincent in the shoulder and he fell to the ground. Ray stood over Gail protecting her from anymore stray shots as she tended to Vincent.

Sahara was shaking Sonny like a rag doll and he dropped the gun. The pure power of the animal was extreme, and Gail screamed for her to let Sonny go. It was too late, Sahara had him by the neck, and with one last gurgle Sonny was dead. All anyone could do was watch; even Terry, Bob, Dave and Mark knew there was nothing that they could do. Eduardo stood frozen all he could see was Sonny lying there dead, his face turned white as a sheet when he knew that he was next, he could no longer hear them telling him to get out of the cage. Sahara turned her head to the other intruder in her cage, and what was worse, she could hear her babies crying for her. With one huge swipe, Sahara slashed through Eduardo's thigh muscle. Dominic was slowly moving into the cage where he knew could be certain death for him, but he could no longer stand and watch. Just as Eduardo thought he was going to die like Sonny, Dominic pulled him out to safety and closed the door with only a second away from death himself. Sahara went back over to Sonny and laid across his lifeless body as if to say, you give me my babies and you can have him.

Roberto fired the tranquilzer dart and hit her in the right hip, and in only seconds, Sahara started to go out again. Roberto and Daniel went in and pulled Sonny out. Gail went to see if she could do anything, but no one could help him now.

At the time everyone else seemed fine, but only to find out that Mark was also shot in the right upper arm. Gail got the bleeding stopped for Vincent, he told her that he had much closer calls than this, somehow Gail believed him. Raymond, please keep that pressure down on your Uncle. Gail went over to check on Mark, his wound was in and out and didn't need much to stop the bleeding. Gail thought that it was a good thing that the zoo kept everything stocked like a hospital does or she would be in trouble. Dominic thought that he would feel good knowing that Sonny was dead, but all he felt was sorrow for both families.

Chapter 50

Bob had called for backup and for an ambulance also, just a little before Sonny was mauled to death, there was no helping him now. They would take Vincent and Mark to the hospital. Mark didn't want to go but, Captain Lane told him, when you get to be Captain, then you can make the calls, until then get your ass in the bus. Dave and Bob started to rope off the area. They had moved Vincent into the ambulance with Mark who was seated on the side. Sonny would have to wait for the coroner. While Sahara was out, Roberto and Daneil brought her into another cage, cleaned the blood off of her and put her babies in with her so when she woke up everything would be fine as far as she knew. It was a different story for the rest of them. Roberto was wondering how he was going to tell Lucinda about Sonny. It was going to be hard on her. Bob and Dave were going around getting everyones statement, but they were all the same. Everyone saw it all, nothing different and nothing else could be done. An open and shut case. Dominic was the only one to take control of the situation when he pulled Eduardo from the cage, which took a lot of guts on his part.

Eduardo was rushed off to the hospital in the first ambulance, he was going to need surgery right away. Gail triaged them in order of their injuries. They could call whom they wanted, but Gail had a feeling that Dominic would also tell Joelina to come with her parents to the hospital. Vincent called for Mark to lean down so he could hear what he had to say. When Mark bent down, Vincent said, if things workout between you and Joelina or not, I would still be proud to call you family, vincent held out his hand and mark shook hands with him. Mark had to turn his head so no one could see the tears in his eyes.

Roberto and Daniel were going to stay and clean up the blood from the cage so the day shift didn't have to see it, they would see enough on the news as it was, then he would go home and talk to his wife. Gail and Ray went to the hospital so Gail could scrub in for surgery if they needed her to. Eduardo would be first. Gail asked Ray who would be calling Eduardo's family and Ray told her that Dominic had already done so. His father Demitri, would be here in the next few hours. Gail hoped that they could finally get this worked out between the two family's.

When Vincent was pulled down the hall, Dominic was with him, this was a very close family and would always be, Gail almost felt a warmth come over her about that. Mark was brought in the same time as Vincent. Captain Lane called Mark's family and they were there waiting for him when he got there. While in the Emergency room, he was talking to his father when he saw Joelina look around the curtain. Mark motioned for her to come over to him. Father, I'd like you to meet Joelina Bertolli, she blushed and shook Mr. Marshall's hand. Very nice to meet you young lady, you too sir, said Joelina, she then went over to Mark and reached out to hug him. Mark, don't you start scarring me right off the bat, you hear me mister, Joelina said with a smile and tears in her eyes.

Dave then came around the curtain and saw that Mark was doing just fine, the shot was through and through the flesh. No arteries were hit at all, he was a lucky man, Dave was very thankful in his heart but said, well as usual, I have to hold up the rest of the team, when are you going to get your lazy butt out of that bed he said as he shook hands with Mark's father James. "When I think he's ready to, said Gail as she walked into the room. Hello everyone Gail said as she was introduced to Mark's father, you have one hell of a son here, I do know that Dr.

McDougal, said James as he shook hands with her. Your Uncle Vincent is in surgery now and just about finished with him, he wasn't as lucky as you, but he will be fine in a couple of weeks or so. Thank God said Joelina, that will please Papa. What about the other man, the one that Joelina's Uncle Dominic pulled out of the cage? How is he?

Eduardo will be fine also, he has some major recovering to do and therapy but, at least he's alive thanks to Dominic. It took a lot of courage to go into that cage and risk his own life to save someone who was trying to do harm to his own family. Dominic truely is a hero said Gail.

Chapter 51

Michael and Christina were at the hospital now to see how everyone was doing. Gail, Michael said, how can we ever do without you in our family again? Well I hope we never have to be without each other now that Ray and I are engaged. Christina came up and hugged her and they both smiled at everyone there.

Gail looked around and was thinking that only an hour ago everything seemed normal. Gail guessed in this family this was normal, she hoped not, because she was marrying Ray no matter what. Ray was with Dominic and some others in the waiting room now. Gail was on her way to let everyone know that all three would be fine, that is all but Sonny.

Gail walked into the waiting room and Ray jumped up to hold her. "Gail, Doctor Harmon said that if you wouldn't have been there that Uncle Vincent could have bled to death." Well, that's where you came in, when I told you to keep pressure on his shoulder, so you helped just as well. Still, said Ray, I don't know how much more this family can take at one time. Gail told them that everyone would be fine, including Eduardo. Mark is in good hands with his father and Joelina with him. "I wondered where she had run off to, said Michael." Vincent should be coming down from surgery at anytime now and then into recovery. It's all going to be fine, really. I just have this feeling, Gail said as she hugged Raymond.

After Roberto and Daniel got everything cleaned up, Roberto told Dan to go home and get a good nights rest because, he would need it in the morning because, he wouldn't be there , he would be with Lucinda and the children all day, and to help his wife to make plans to get Sonny home to Sicily. Roberto went out and took one last look at Sahara and her cubs. They were all cuddled up and sleeping. Roberto couldn't help but think that had it not been for Sahara, Sonny probably would have killed him. That's something he decided that he would never think about again. He walked out to his car to go home to see his wife and to let those policeman go home to their family's also.

Mark asked Joelina if he would still get that first date. Joelina smiled and said, now more than ever, you helped save my family, and to a Bertolli that means everything. Mark's father had gone down to get some coffee, so Joelina reached up and kissed him and said, that's just in case you don't get around to do that soon, she smiled. "Do you mind?" Not at al Mark said, can I have another? Absolutly my hero, Joelina was glad that his father had stepped out for a moment because she gave him a kiss that he would long remember.

Roberto got home and the police officers had already talked to Captain Lane, they were just waiting for him to come home before they left. Roberto shook their hands and thanked them for all their help as he walked them to the door. Lucinda was coming down the stairs from putting the children to bed. Roberto walked up to her and held her very close, she held him closer. "Roberto, what is wrong?" Come and sit down here by me on the sofa Lucinda, I have a lot to tell you about what happened tonight. "Are the leopards all fine, nothing went bad did it?" This isn't about the leopards, well in a way it is. This is about Sonny. "Sonny, was Sonny at the zoo, cried Lucinda?" Yes, he was along with Eduarto Gianti, his friend from Sicily. Yes, I know who Eduardo is, what is wrong Roberto?

Lucinda, there is no easy way to tell you this but, Sonny came to the zoo tonight to kill me. "No, cried Lucinda, as she held Roberto's hand tighter." Sonny and Eduardo walked into the cage after I had sedated Sahara and she was down in the hay, Daniel and I had the cubs, weighing them and checking them over when Sonny walked up to us before we knew what was happening. Ray and Gail along with four police men, kept telling Sonny and Eduardo to get out of there. Sonny wouldn't listen and he just kept screaming louder and louder. Sahara was coming out of sedation, it all happend so fast, Sonny never had a chance, it was too late. "What do you mean too late, what are you trying to say Roberto?" I'm saying that Sonny is dead, Sahara got to him before I had a chance to hit her again with the next dart, he thought that I was going to shoot him and wouldn't let me even raise the gun up to shoot Sahara. "Oh no, Roberto cried Lucinda, my brother is dead?" Why was he so mad at us that he wanted to kill you?" Lucinda, Sonny was the one who tried to kill my father, and took the shot that could have killed Joelina. Lucinda dropped down in front of Roberto and layed her head in his lap and cried, I'm so ashamed of my family, I will spend the rest of my life trying to make it up to you and your family. Sonny was the last of my family, so you never have to fear us again. Roberto pulled Lucinda up to her feet and told her that there was nothing for her to make up for. No one in my family blames you for any of this or Sonny, really. Sonny has not been right for some time now honey, and if you search your feelings you know that I am right said Roberto.

Roberto then began at the beginning of the evening and brought her up to the present time. So much has happened in such a short time, but things will die down in time. Eduardo's father is flying in sometime in the early morning around ten o'clock, I would like to be there to talk with him, would you mind if I go alone first? My husband, you may do whatever makes you happy, but I would like to talk to Eduardo myself before he leaves to go home, if that's okay? I just want to ask him, what ticked Sonny off so bad to want to do this to my family, and try and understand it all. I may never understand it. I love you Lucinda, let's go to bed, I'm very tired. I love you too Roberto. I will have to make arrangements for Sonny to get back home, where he can be laid next to Papa. I will need you to help me with Mama Roberto, this will break her heart. Yes dear, you know that I will. I told the coroner that we would be in sometime tomorrow to make the arrangements. Now we need sleep, and they walked up the stairs together hand in hand.

Chapter 52

Ray and Gail said their goodnights after she had checked on everyone involved in this evening's events. When they walked out to the parking garage, Ray stopped and just held onto her so tight, she had to tell him that he was crushing her. "I'm sorry sweetheart, but I couldn't help but think about, what if it had been you that was shot tonight, who would have saved you?" "You would have Ray, I have no doubt about that, whatever it would have taken, you would have done it, that's how much I trust you." I don't ever want to try that kind of trust out again, if you don't mind, Ray said. They went over and got into Ray's car, but before they could get off of the hospital property, Gail's beeper went off. It was Mr. Kadell, she would have to go back in again. Why don't you have a bath drawn for me in a half hour after you get home, then we can get in it together, how does that sound? How will you get home, your car is at my house? I'll call a cab, and I'll only be a half an hour behind you. "You got it kiddo, a hot tub and a hot man to go with it coming right up." I hope so, Gail kissed him and went back into the hospital.

Everyone left for home except for Dominic, he stayed with Vincent As it happened they put Eduardo and Vincent in the same room to recover until the morning, Dominic would watch them both. He couldn't help but feel sorry for the young man, you could tell that he was afraid of his own shadow, and that Sonny was the leader of the two, but Dominic would still be careful with this family

Gail walked up to the second floor nurses station to find out what was going on with Mr. Kadell. Margie was still there from the day shift, someone called off and she got stuck with having to stay. Margie told Gail that he was fine when I went to check on him at dinner, but when I checked again at nine, his face was flushed, he had a slight fever and was starting to get a rash on him. Gail read the report, Gary's blood pressure and his pulse was both up too high. "He's asking for his "Sweet Pea", so I called you, said Margie. I'm sorry, I hear that you have had your hands full tonight as it is. It's alright, you know that Mr. Kadell is my favorite patient anyway, just don't tell the others. They walked down the hall together laughing. Gail walked into Gary's room and he was not doing very well at all, she told Margie to get a lot of cold packs in here to get his fever down. Gary looked at Gail and said, am I checking out Doc? You look like an angel to me all the time, so I can't tell right now. I think if we get your fever down that we should be okay. "Why do you think that you get these fevers all the time Gary?" I can tell by the labs that your white cell count is up, but no reason as of why. I know that you don't like to talk about when you were in Vietnam, but have you had these problems off and on since then? "Yes Doc, I think I still might have the clap, what do you think?" I think that we would have known about that a long time ago from all the blood work that we have done. "How does this feel, Gail said as she pushed on his right lower abdomen." "Shit Doc, what are you trying to do, kill me off, that hurts. "I think that your having an appendix attack. Margie came in with the ice packs and they put them on his lower abdomen and pelvic area. "Now, if this cools down, we are probably going in there tomorrow and take that out." Well I guess I'll see you in the morning Sweet Pea. Yes, and you know that I love you more than my luggage also. Gail laughed with him, I'll see you in the morning. Gail walked back to the station desk and told Margie that if anything changed to let her know. Gail also left instructions for Margie to call in Dr. Harmon to scrub in for Mr. Kadell for 7 am, and to call her if anything changes.

Now to her hot bath, with the hot man that she loved. Gail caught a cab and was at Ray's in no time at all. Gail walked in and sweet music was playing on the stereo, and candles were lit everywhere, there was no need to even turn on a light. Gail stripped as she walked down the hall to the bathroom. When she turned and walked into the bathroom, Ray was just getting into the tub himself. Ray also had wine chilling in a bucket and rose petals in the tub. Ray looked over to Gail and saw her naked and froze halfway into the tub, she was so amazing and beautiful. Gail walked into the room and got into the tub also. Ray poured her a glass of wine and gave it to her. Gail took a sip and it was wonderful . Ray began to rub her feet to relax her. "Oh Ray, said Gail, you have no idea of how much I love you, and more than I knew until this very moment, I think that I do love you more everyday." I know that it's not possible to love you more, but I do every single day. Ray just smiled and the rest of the night was perfect.

Chapter 53

Michael and Christina were at the hospital bright and early this morning to see Vincent, Mark and Eduardo before they went to open the store. As they were walking down the isle to the rooms, they say Mark's father come out of the room. "How is our hero doing today, asked Michael?" He is doing fine, they plan to release him this afternoon. Your daughter is a wonderful lady, and I can see why my son is so infatuated with her. She feels the same way I believe said Christina. She will be here in just a moment, she is parking the car for her old parents, they all three laughed at that. Well, it was nice to meet you and I'm sure that we will be meeting again. I am off to work myself, so you all have a nice day, goodbye. Goodbye to you too sir.

They went in to see Mark first and were very delighted to find him in good shape. "It will take more than a small shot like that to keep me down Mark said." Is Joelina at the store? "Where else would you think she should be son?" Michael just smiled, he could see the look of dissapointment on Mark's face, but before he could tell him, Joelina came to the door. Mark's face lit up like a Christmas tree and so did Joelina's. "Yes, I think love is in the air, thought Christina." Michael and herself would leave the love birds alone. Come by our house tonight for dinner son, we would be proud to have you. Thank you sir, I'd like that. They have barely made it out of the room, before Mark pulled Joelina tight and repaid the kiss from last night. "Well someone is feeling much better today, said Joelina."

When Michael and Christina were getting close to Vincent's room, they saw Dominic coming out of the room, he saw them and told them that Mr. Gianti was in seeing his son, Eduardo. Vincent was still asleep. The three of them went into the waiting room and had some coffee. "Michael; the next time I come for a visit, do you think that we could leave hospitals out of it?" Yes, definatly I agree, and so do I said Christina.

Mr. Gianti came out of the room in thirty minutes or so, he was looking for Michael and found him in the waiting room. May I speak with you gentlemen please? Christina stood and said that she would go and check on the two men, and then she left the room. "I would first like to thank you Dominic for saving my sons life, words cannot express my deepest emotions about that." Eduardo has told me of what a horrible time it was in that cage, and that you risked your own life to pull my son from certain death. I can never say thank you enough. "Now, Michael; I'd like for our families to no longer be enemies." Even though we have not seen each other in years, Eduardo told me what Sonny had told him, and most of it is, I'm sure a lie. Do you think our families could become friends or at least be cordial with one another? I'm quite sure that is how it should be Demitri, and now we will shake on it. All three men shook hands and the feud was over, and things could now get better.

When the men walked into Vincent and Eduardo's room, Vincent was now awake and talking to Eduardo. Do not blame yourself Eduardo; Sonny has not been a stable man for some time now. "I found that out when he wanted me to take a shot at your niece, and I couldn't do it, it is not in me to kill another living being, said Eduardo." We just want you to get better so you can go home with your Papa, said Christina. Demitri Gianti went over and shook Vincent's hand, and then told his son that he needed to go and call his mother so she would stop worrying about you. Tell Mama I'm just fine Papa, and that I'll see her soon. Mr. Gianti, left the room with a wave of his hand goodbye. Michael and Christina said their goodbyes also they had to get to the store, but first they would have to drag Joelina out of Mark's room.

Gail was coming out of surgery with Mr. Kadell, when she saw them coming down the hall and was glad to see their smiling faces. "How is everyone this wonderful morning?" They stood and talked about how everyone was and Christina wanted Gail and Raymond to come over for dinner also. Gail said that they would have to decline, Ray had to work and Gail needed to be home for her daughter to come home. I had almost forgotten about that, well you have a wonderful time at dinner on Wednesday. We will see you soon Gail, we have to remove Joelina out of Mark's room. Gail walked into the room and saw both men sitting up and drinking some 7-up. "Well you both look better than the last time that I saw you." Vincent held out his hand and said to Gail, I can never thank you enough for saving me last night, Both Eduardo and myself want to say thank you, then Vincent pulled Gail down and kissed her on both cheeks, Gail blushed. "Yes, please accept my heartfelt thanks for saving my life also said Eduardo. My doctor said that if you had not of put that tourniquet on my leg that I would not have made it to the hospital, and for that I am totally grateful." You are both very welcome. You doctor says that he is going to let you go home maybe by next Thursday, and you Uncle Vincent, will probably go home tomorrow or the next day. How does that sound? At the same time they both said wonderful.

Gail's office manager and nurse Pat, came in to talk to Gail about the mornings patient load and she could not stop starring at Dominic. Pat? Pat, are you alright? Oh, yes I'm sorry doctor, here is your schedule, and then she stumbled out of the room. Gail got up and said her goodbyes and went out into the hall. She heard Vincent teasing Dominic about Pat. Dominic said that she was a very nice looking lady. Gail just smiled.

Gail would talk to Ray, but she wanted to invite Dominic and Pat to dinner with her son and daughter, and maybe Joelina and Mark. You could see it was love at first sight with those two, and who knows, maybe her's and Ray's wouldn't be the only wedding coming up. Gail thought back on something that her mother used to say; "There are four things that you can't recover: A stone after it is thrown, a word after it is said, the occasion after it is missed, and the time after it is gone." Gail would no longer think or worry about people from her past, there's a reason why they didn't make it to the future. Gail always wanted a man that would come into her life on accident, but stayed on purpose, and that was Ray.

Gail had another surprise for Ray when they got back to Ray's house. Gail would be the one to run the bath water this time; she would also set the little bear on the pillows on the bed. Gail already knew that the color was blue, as in positive on the EPT test that she took yesterday when Ray was waiting for her to go to his parents' house for dinner. She had only looked at it this morning while Ray was still sleeping. She would tell him tonight.

One child for Ray would be a delight for everyone, especially Gail herself, because secretly she did want one more child. Now they would both get their wish. Yes, "Sweet Pea" was full of joy.....